EVIL WOMAN!

Longarm threw open the shutter on his bull's eye lamp to sweep its beam through the forest of uprights betwixt them and the distant line of other lights. The banshee's inhuman wails echoed and re-echoed to where you just couldn't say where they were coming from. Hearing them for the second time, Longarm suspected they might not be so loud, as a matter of volume, as they were shrill as a matter of nerve-tingle, the way fingernails scraping a blackboard set everyone's teeth on edge way more than a locomotive whistle could, blowing at a lower note . . .

Then Longarm caught the banshee full in his beam, like a jacklighted deer. Only no deer had ever stared so wildly into a beam of light from under a wild mop of gray hair, waving its arms above the same, dressed in a tattered graveyard shroud, knee-deep in white mist.

"Hold it right there or I'll shoot!" Longarm yelled as he advanced on the unearthly whatever while it went on hollering at him . . .

DON'T MISS THESE
ALL-ACTION WESTERN SERIES
FROM THE BERKLEY PUBLISHING GROUP

THE GUNSMITH by J. R. Roberts
Clint Adams was a legend among lawmen, outlaws, and ladies. They called him . . . the Gunsmith.

LONGARM by Tabor Evans
The popular long-running series about U.S. Deputy Marshal Long—his life, his loves, his fight for justice.

SLOCUM by Jake Logan
Today's longest-running action Western. John Slocum rides a deadly trail of hot blood and cold steel.

BUSHWHACKERS by B. J. Lanagan
An action-packed series by the creators of Longarm! The rousing adventures of the most brutal gang of cutthroats ever assembled—Quantrill's Raiders.

TABOR EVANS

LONGARM

AND THE BLOSSOM ROCK BANSHEE

JOVE BOOKS, NEW YORK

LONGARM AND THE BLOSSOM ROCK BANSHEE

A Jove Book / published by arrangement with
the author

PRINTING HISTORY
Jove edition / October 1998

The Penguin Putnam Inc. World Wide Web site address is
http://www.penguinputnam.com

ISBN: 0-515-12372-2

A JOVE BOOK®
Jove Books are published by The Berkley Publishing Group, a member
of Penguin Putnam Inc.,
375 Hudson Street, New York, New York 10014.
JOVE and the "J" design are trademarks
belonging to Jove Publications, Inc.

PRINTED IN THE UNITED STATES OF AMERICA

10 9 8 7 6 5 4 3 2 1

LONGARM

AND THE BLOSSOM ROCK BANSHEE

Chapter 1

When you're driving steel with a nine-pound hammer you get more noise than results. So when Grogan on the star-drill cried, "Lave off! I hear something!" the muscular Flannery, swinging the sledge while dressed in nothing but his shoes, breechclout, and a dusty coat of sweat, struck again and jeered, "Of course you hear something, you great loon! There's divvel a man working the Comstock Lode that can hammer as loud as meself!"

Grogan rotated the heavy steel bar he was gripping as he insisted, "I wasn't speaking of your gentle tapping, Sean Flannery. It was back there in the blackness of the gallery I was hearing somebody treading where nobody else should be treading!"

Before they could argue further, Sixty Cent Sullivan, the blaster and nominal head of the three-man crew, cut in saying, "Shove a sock in it and finish that last hole before our time in this tribute is up! I want to be after blasting and mucking before they change shifts down below and jump at the chance to fire us for showing up late on the job!"

Grogan sighed and said, "You heard the man, Sean Flannery. Why would you just be standing there at a time like this? Is it a statue of the long-dead Chuchulain you'd be posing for?"

1

Flannery said something very rude in Gaelic and struck a mighty blow as Sixty Cent Sullivan, stripped to the waist but wearing pants and a cap with a Davy lamp clipped to it, fished out a pocket watch for an uneasy glance at the hour. The three of them were working tribute on their own time, and he hadn't spoken in jest when he'd said Consolidated was looking for any chance to lay off more workers and the Knights of Labor be damned.

The three men working the blossom rock at one end of an abandoned upper drift were doing nothing illegal or without the knowledge of the Consolidated syndicate by mining the last of a once-mighty ore body. The three were drilling by hand between shifts because they had leased the unworked face of blossom rock from the company by agreeing to share any color they got the hard way, with old-fashioned methods no hardrock company paying as high as four dollars a shift for drilling solid quartz with Burleigh air drills could see enough profit in.

You couldn't use a modern Burleigh in blossom rock, the rotten quartz laced with flecks of native gold and silver where the mother lode melted into country rock to form a sort of bread crust a few yards thick. So the company allowed tribute mining on shares, and given the size of the Comstock Lode, that left an awesome amount of blossom rock for those willing to risk the time, the labor, and perhaps their lives in places where the company had posted dangers signs. For at this stage of its fading glory, the Comstock Lode was a sorry mess.

Discovered halfway up the granite dome called Mount Davidson back in '59 and named for old Hank Comstock, a claim-jumping rogue who'd died broke, by his own hand, back in '70, the Comstock Lode had been about the biggest solid lump of high-grade ore ever worked by mortal man.

Shaped something like a slice of bacon, better than two miles long, fifty to eighty feet thick, and standing on edge from its outcrops to the four-mile Sutro drainage tunnel three thousand feet below, the big slab of blue quartz laced with silver and gold had paid the way for the Union during the

Civil War with a constant stream of wagons crawling like ants along the trail to Frisco Bay a hundred and fifty rugged miles to the west. They were loaded with crude twenty-pound ingots worth fifteen hundred to three thousand dollars apiece, depending on the gold content when they were further refined by the U.S. Mint.

The earliest mining, much like the boomtown of Virginia City, which sprawled along the line of fifteen surface shafts along the slopes of the mountain, had been a slapdash, get-rich-quick business until a series of cave-ins and even more disastrous underground fires had conspired with the Great Depression of the 1870's to drop mining stock to a dollar a share and turn the happy-go-lucky game into a serious business.

Since that time the twelve to fifteen separate mining companies at work on and off had consolidated into one centrally managed syndicate to clean out what was left of the high-grade in a more professional manner.

Black powder had given way to dynamite. Hand drilling was replaced by the big Burleigh drills slung from screw-jack rests and powered by compressed air. And probably best of all, the helter-skelter pit props of the earlier mines had been replaced by a uniform framing system an engineer named Deidesheimer had invented.

Precut timbers, designed to interlock without any need of fasteners, formed the edges of six-foot cubes, with their eighteen-inch uprights and cross-beams of ponderosa or sugar pine stripped from the higher Sierras to the west. Thick planks formed ceilings and floors in the drifts as they extended deeper, with other cubes filled in with waste rock to form massive load-bearing pillars, until, by this time, there were at least a hundred and fifty miles of galleries, shafts, and ramps filling most of the space the original ore body had occupied more solidly. To call this termite pile two miles long, fifty to eighty feet wide, and three thousand feet up and down a maze would be to call Paris, France, a French village.

But all things must come to an end, even when they're being run by gents with engineering degrees. So there were less than a thousand men working underground these days, and only old-timers remembered those bonanza times when a crew leader could draw as much as five dollars a shift. And the three partners working blossom rock on speculation were hoping against hope for blossoms of gold dust as they got ready to blast and muck. The amount of silver they could win by such methods at the current market price of silver would barely pay for the Nobel-Sixty-Percent they'd paid for out of their own pockets. Tribute miners who helped themselves to company supplies didn't get to go down that company's shafts anymore.

Sixty Cent Sullivan, so called because he favored the more dangerous but effective top grade of dynamite, told his drilling crew that last hole was deep enough, and added, "Yez had better move back at least a hundred yards. For the side walls pinch tighter at this end, and there may come a trumpet blast indade!"

To which the muscular Flannery replied with a scowl, "Aroo, and why don't you go home and comfort your dear old mother, who hasn't had a good diddle since yourself and the pig ran away!"

Sixty Cent Sullivan was a man who perforce lived dangerously. So he quietly removed his cap and set it on the dynamite box with the beam of his Davy lamp bouncing off the floor planks as he almost purred, "And would you care to rephrase that last remark, or would you rather spend the rest of your short life with no balls, Sean Flannery?"

The much bigger Flannery set his nine-pound sledge aside and might have said anything, if the three of them had not heard a loose rock falling down, down, and then down some more through the darkness all around.

Grogan gasped, "Jasus, Mary, and Joseph, and I told yez I'd heard a footstep or worse in this tribute, where nobody else has permission to be!"

Flannery snatched up his hammer and called out, "Who's there? What do you want? Show yourself before I smash your

4

head, you high-grading son of a one-legged whore and a Gypsy chicken thief!''

Sixty Cent warned, ''Whist! Watch your step, you great ox! There's no flooring over that way for anyone to be after trespassing along! Just the open framework against a good thousand-foot hanging wall! Rocks do fall by themselves. It's the nature of rocks to fall, and I thought we was about to have a fight.''

Grogan stepped between them with his steel star-drill held at port arms across his own naked chest as he said, ''I thought we was after some blossom, and why are yez at each other's throats when I could be getting rich?''

Sixty Cent growled, ''He mentioned me mother.''

To which Flannery replied in a defensive tone, ''After you ordered me about like a greenhorn off the Boston boat! I've been driving steel as long as any man here pulled his first shift underground, and I'll not be told where to go or how to hold me dick while the great man is lighting his firecrackers!''

Grogan said soothingly, ''We're all bone-weary and worried about the same thing, if any man here would care to say the word. Come with me, Sean, and let the dear man make us rich.''

As they turned away, Sixty Cent called after them, ''What about me mother?''

Flannery laughed, but resisted the temptation. Grogan called back that the remark had only been made in jest, and since Flannery didn't say that was a lie, Sixty Cent Sullivan shrugged and turned back to the face to charge, fuse, and tamp the sixteen holes in the blossom rock.

He worked fast, suddenly feeling more alone than he usually did at a time when the shooter was supposed to be working alone. Just as the mines of Montana were worked by Cornish Cousin Jacks, while the western slope of the Sierra Nevada employed a lot of Italian-Swiss, the Comstock Lode employed mostly Irish hardrockers because the bonanza barons who'd first dug into the Comstock Lode had been Fair, Flood, Mackay, and O'Brian, all Irish-born and inclined to feel more comfortable with their own kind. But while Irishmen were blessed with plenty of energy, they were inclined to have been raised on stories of things that went bump in the dark. And hadn't poor Tom Corrigan said he'd heard the banshee wailing in the old Ophir diggings, and hadn't all that rock sat down on Tom just a few days later to be turning him into raspberry jam they had to bury in an oil drum and all?

Sixty Cent told himself to grow up as he fused the last charge and tamped it with clay. Nobody else had heard Corrigan's banshee, and if *he'd* heard it at all, his own worried mind had been warning him about that poorly shored rock before it had ever come loose. Tales of the *ban na n'sitheach,* the fairy's wife, or some pagan prophetess called a *banfhaidh,* depending on whose grandmother one asked, made for nightmares on stormy nights and uneasy feelings a thousand feet under the ground where the fairy folk and worse were said to dwell.

As he braided the sixteen fuses together and struck a match to light the train, the man who'd never actually heard the banshee reflected that you never did unless it was yourself or someone close to you that the banshee was warning with her cries. So he yelled, "Fire in the hole!" and chased the beam of his Davy lamp back along the gallery until he came upon Grogan and Flannery, crouched behind the massive pillar of pine where four Deidesheimer frames had been tightly wedged together by the pressure from all sides.

As Sixty Cent dropped down on one knee with them, Flannery dryly but sweetly inquired whether he'd thought to light the fuses.

He was answered by a deep hollow-throated cough, and the framing all around them tingled like the plucked strings of a thousand bass violins. Then the three of them heard the rumble and patter of the falling blossom rock, and Grogan chortled, "It's two tons or more we have to be after mucking for color, and should this big mick ever lay a hand on you, your mother, or her pig, I'll be hitting him with this very star-drill for yez!"

The three partners laughed and rose in restored good humor

to head back. Sixty Cent warned, ''Not too fast, lads. We don't want to start our shift down below with nitro headaches, and it's best to let the air be clearing closer to the face.''

Then he added, ''What the hell?'' as his Davy beam bounced back at them from a swirling wall of white mist a good thirty yards in front of the modest blast he'd just set off.

''White damp?'' asked Grogan in a worried tone.

To which Flannery replied, ''Don't be daft! You get white damp in a *coal* measure! This is a hardrock mine and where would white damp be coming from in solid rock and all?''

Sixty Cent sniffed and volunteered, ''Doesn't smell wet, but that could be steam from another hot spring. Wouldn't be the first boiling water anyone's drilled into under Mount Davidson, you know.''

As they slowly advanced with their tools and experience, Flannery decided, ''It must be a hot spring, and wasn't that a foin deed for Mr. Adolph Sutro to be after doing just a year or so ago, driving that grand drainage tunnel in from the desert flats to the east to be draining all that water, hot and cold, we've been drilling into faster than anything but Sir Isaac Newton's grand laws could get rid of!''

''That's not steam,'' Sixty Cent declared.

Before anyone could ask him what he thought it was, the three of them were rooted in place, neck hairs atingle, by the sound of a human voice suddenly screaming gibberish or sobbing higher and higher, then even higher, until it felt like fingernails scraping on slate in a range a coyote would have found painful—if any mortal coyote ever managed to yell like that.

''Jasus, Mary, and Joseph!'' wailed Grogan in return as the muscular Flannery raised his nine-pound hammer and called out, ''Lave off all that yammering or there'll be some hammering! Show yourself and tell us what you want before I swat you like a fly!''

Whatever it was lowered its wails to ghastly moans, followed by a cackle of laughter and another impossibly shrill wail that bounced back and forth between the rock walls in the darkness to either side.

Flannery waded into the swirling mist with his hammer held high as Sixty Cent called out, "Don't do it, Sean! You have to see where you'd be planting a foot in this played-out drift! A lot of the flooring has been salvaged for other works!"

Whether Flannery heard the warning above the wailing or not was moot, for just as the voice sank back down to a gibbering cackle, they heard Flannery scream in turn, a long fading scream as he fell down and then down some more through open latticework bracing the blossom rock of the western wall, until all they could hear were lingering echoes in the darkness.

Sixty Cent crossed himself and sobbed, "I told him not to risk such a fall and you heard me tell him, Grogan!"

But Grogan wasn't there to answer, and as the banshee began to wail again, Sixty Cent was chasing his beam for the nearest ladder shaft, bawling like a lost lamb. And then his cap fell off and he had no light and he didn't care as he grasped the ladder rungs to scamble down into the darkness for as far down as the ladder still ran.

And then there were no ladder rungs where ladder rungs should have been, and then Sixty Cent Sullivan was screaming, all the way down the thousand-foot shaft, until the sobbing Grogan, pissing his pants as he clung to a more solid ladder in the blackness, couldn't hear anything but that maddening banshee wailing in the dark.

Chapter 2

Marshal William Vail of the Denver Federal District Court did not believe in banshees. Even if he had, he wouldn't have had jurisdiction over a banshee wailing in a Nevada mine. So he'd dispatched his U.S. Deputy Marshal Custis Long to Virginia City on another matter entirely.

Getting there from Denver could be a bother.

You had to change trains three times, and still get off at Reno to board the Wells Fargo stagecoach south along the eastern slopes of the Sierra Nevada, which rose steeper and starker on that side as it teased the sage and salt flats of the vast and dry Great Basin with the sight of summer snow still lingering on the higher peaks.

Wells Fargo ran first-class stage lines where the iron horse just wouldn't carry folks. But that wasn't saying much next to traveling by rail this late in the reign of Queen Victoria. So by the time they'd rolled into the relay station called Steamboat, the six southbound passengers were uniformly coated with mustard-colored dust and the one lady on board, a petite brunette when she'd first gotten on in what had been a polka-dot blue sunbonnet and slate-gray travel duster, was busting a gut not to throw up.

The tall and once-tan Longarm, as he was better known to friend and foe alike, was wearing a tobacco-tweed outfit and a coffee-brown Stetson with a Colorado crush under his own coating of mustard dust. He didn't suspect the lady cared what he'd once looked like as he leaned forward to gently suggest, "I'd be proud to swap seats and let you ride sitting forwards, ma'am. We ain't stopping here long enough to buy you no ginger beer. But I got me some dinner mints left over from the dining car on that Central Pacific varnish we got off back in Reno."

She didn't answer, and turned to stare out the window as the Wells Fargo station hands changed teams. Longarm didn't crane his neck to look. He knew how you changed teams, and nobody did it better or quicker than the old pros left in an ever-shrinking line of work. The ox-team drivers still hauling freight where the rails had yet to be laid were inclined to be more sober and more expert with their bullwhips than a teamster had been required to be on the recently closed Santa Fe Trail.

A laconic hatchet-faced gent, who Longarm had taken for a gambling man or a whiskey drummer back when he'd been sporting a pearl-gray Stetson and maroon brocade vest under a funeral-black frock coat, chuckled fondly and quietly remarked, "Nice try, cowboy," as the three other passengers pretended not to hear. For a man who twitted a stranger packing a Colt double-action .44-40 cross-draw was either a dangerously foolish greenhorn or somebody even more dangerous.

Longarm had outgrown keeping score on either the men or the women he'd tangled with since he'd kissed his first gal and killed his first man before he'd been old enough to vote. So he just stared out his own window at nothing much, until the hatchet face seated catty-corner from him said, "I was talking to you, cowboy. Has the cat got your tongue, or did your momma warn you not to talk to strangers when you were out of her sight?"

By this time the fresh mules had been hitched up and they were off with no ceremony, save for the crack of the jehu's whip and a sickening lurch as the heavily laden cab of their Concord chased after its own undercarriage on its oxhide thoroughbraces, inspiring Longarm to grab for the upright door jamb ahead of him as the dusty gal ahead of him doubled over till her sunbonnet bobbed between their facing knees. He would have suggested she puke out the window if they'd been on speaking terms. But they weren't, and what the hell, he was going to have to wash his boots off at the end of the line in any case.

As the coach settled around them to as steady a side-to-side roll as the wagon trace to Virginia City allowed, the gal sat up, looking as if she'd been roped and dragged at least a furlong backwards, and timidly asked, "Could I please have one of those mints you mentioned, kind sir?"

Longarm reached in his coat for the empty envelope he'd stuffed with dining car mints aboard their train as that same sardonic cuss laughed and said, "There you go, cowboy. I was wondering why you were playing the strong silent type. The ladies seem to fall for that. I've never understood how come. Why don't you tell us, Romeo?"

Longarm handed the mints across to the gal, murmuring, "Don't chaw. Let 'em melt in your mouth one at a time as you stare out at the far horizon. Don't pay attention to nothing closer until your eyes and your innards settle on which ways are up and down."

She took the mints with a nod of thanks, and popped three between her dusty lips as their hatchet-faced fellow traveler jeered, "Romeo, Romeo, wherefore art thou, Romeo?"

Longarm opened the centerfire door and rose, then rose some more with his head and shoulders out and almost at rump level with their driver as he called, "Rein in for a moment in the name of the law, gents. I'd be the law and we seem to have a public menace to deal with down here!"

It took some hauling back and one instep on the brake lever, but they ground to a halt soon enough, and before the coach had come to a complete halt, Longarm had dropped to the caliche crust just off the trail and called in, "It's time to come out and play now, tinhorn!"

There came an ominous moment of silence before that same

sarcastic voice called back, "Are you talking to me? Have you lost your reason and your will to live? Don't you know who I am?"

To which Longarm replied, "I don't care who you am. I just want you to step out here with me and say you're sorry or fill your fist. That momma you made the mistake of mentioning raised me never to swat flies where others might get hurt!"

The hitherto-jeering voice seemed more polite as it replied in an attempt at banter, "Oh, for Pete's sake, can't you take a joke?"

Longarm didn't try to sound any different as he calmly replied, "No. When I want to fight with a man I just tell him. I don't make snide comments about things that ain't none of my business. If you want to fight me, step down from that coach and let's have it over with. If you don't want to fight me, step down from that coach anyhow and tell me how sorry you are."

The jehu called down, "That's enough for now, gents. I got to get this coach in to Virginia and, no offense, the two of you are talking silly!"

Longarm called back, "You drive off without me and I'll look you up the next time you drive this route again! I am a U.S. deputy marshal on an official mission, and the public menace I aim to rid you of has said mean things about my momma and other ladies in front of witnesses!"

A voice that had been silent up to then called out, "The lawman has called it true, jehu. I'd be Nat Rothfeld of Gould & Curry in Virginia, and I've got the drop on this public menace in here! He got on spoiling for a fight, and I'd fight him myself if that deputy hadn't seen him first!"

That seemed to inspire other remarks from the other male passengers, and then the sarcastic gent with the hatchet face was climbing down from the coach to grin sheepishly and bleat, "For Pete's sake, I was *joshing*!"

Longarm said, "I heard you. Heard you say something about being a big bad boo I didn't want to mess with too. I'd be U.S. Deputy Marshal Custis Long of the Denver Federal District Court. Now that I've shown you mine, suppose you show me yours."

The man who'd started up with him for no just reason sighed and said, "I'd be Jefferson Otis. I work for the Pinkerton Detective Agency."

Longarm flatly replied, "Not no more. I've heard of you and know your brag, Jeff Otis. You were fired from the Pinks for gunning that Chinaman in Wyoming for reasons best known to yourself. So who are you really riding for, and won't you *please* go for that famous Colt Lightning in that famous shoulder holster?"

The defrocked Pinkerton man kept his hands very polite as he told Longarm, "I had reason to suspect that Chinee was pestering a white lady aboard that train that evening. If you aim to be picky, I'm sort of working on my own out of Reno these days. They just wired me about some funny business down in the Consolidated Comstock holdings. How was I supposed to know you were another lawman?"

Longarm snorted in disgust and growled, "You can call a hound's tail its fifth leg, and you can call a born bully a lawman, but you still have a hound's tail and a born bully. As for how you're supposed to know who a man might be before you mess with him, you *ask* before you mess with him. Might have saved that Chinese diplomat and the Union Pacific line a heap of trouble if you'd bothered to find out who he was before you gunned him so bravely in a first-class Pullman."

Longarm stepped around Otis without turning his back on the known killer, and hauled himself half aboard the coach again before he called out, "Drive on, jehu. I just put out the garbage for you!"

As the driver hesitated, Otis took one step toward the coach before he found himself staring into a muzzle bored for .44-40 and heard the man holding it say not unkindly, "Stay where you are or I'll kill you as gently as you killed that unarmed Chinaman."

13

"You can't leave me here in the desert!" Otis wailed even as the jehu cracked his whip.

As the coach lurched forward again, Longarm called back conversationally, "Sure we can. It ain't pure desert. There's water in them hills to the west and it's only another eight or ten miles to Virginia!"

Then he stayed put with one foot inside and the other on the brass step as he told the motion-sick brunette, "Get yourself in that other seat and riding to face forward, ma'am. I mean you no harm, and I won't say another word after we have you and your innards riding sensibly!"

One of the older gents inside told her to do as she was told. So she half rose, and Longarm steadied her as she swung her shapely rump around to plop in a cloud of dust where he'd been seated before.

Longarm took her seat. He didn't like to ride backwards, but there was only another hour's ride to suffer through and he'd ridden backwards farther without puking.

The passenger who'd identified himself as working for the mining syndicate was a tad older and dressed fancier than Longarm could afford. As they got to rolling, he smiled through the dust on his own mustache and said, "That old boy is surely going around the bend. It gets worse every time he starts up with some total stranger. I figured he'd know better than to start up with *me* because we've been pointed out to one another in Reno and wolves would as soon not hunt one another in a world so filled with sheep."

Longarm put his six-gun away with a thin smile and said, "I don't mind being called a sheep as long as nobody mentions my dear old momma. I had no idea who he was until he bragged on his name and a rep that really ain't worth bragging about. I take it you pack a gun for Gould & Curry?"

Rothfeld shook his head and modestly replied, "Accounting department. You don't have to be a gunfighter when you run with the biggest wolf pack on this slope of the Sierras. So I wasn't being heroic just now. I knew he knew I worked for

14

the senior partners in the Comstock Consolidation and he hasn't gone completely crazy yet.''

The other passenger who'd spoken to the motion-sick brunette was a portly gent whose full beard had been white when he'd first gotten on in Reno. He said, ''To be frank, I was afraid for all of us when that mad dog began to growl. I've had Jeff Otis pointed out to me as well, and mark my words, he's on his way to Virginia to kill somebody for a modest fee, if not for practice!''

Nat Rothfeld shrugged and volunteered, ''Things have been quiet down our way of late. A lot of men have been laid off, and you naturally get rid of the troublemakers first.''

''What about that banshee haunting those abandoned Ophir drifts?'' the older, bearded man suggested.

The accountant caught Longarm's quizzical glance and shrugged. ''An unfortunate combination of some crazy lady wandering around in the dark and shanty Irish superstition.''

The petite brunette sucking after-dinner mints kept her eyes on the far horizon, having discovered that it helped, but couldn't resist making a public declaration that went, ''If a certain gentleman of the Hebrew persuasion might care to know, I happen to be an Irish Catholic and I do not consider my faith a superstition!''

''Nor do I, ma'am!'' the accountant gallantly assured her, adding in a more soothing tone, ''I wasn't speaking of Irish people of *quality*. I was simply relating the sad tale of three ignorant immigrants, two of them no longer with us, who thought they'd heard that notorious Irish banshee whom, it's safe to say, the Church of Rome has never recognized as anything but a peasant superstition.''

The brunette replied in a somewhat mollified tone, ''In that case I was referring to your own faith with the greatest respect, kind sir.''

Longarm asked, ''What happened to the two that are no longer with us?''

The mining company man made a wry face and explained, ''Both killed in about the same way. Don't ever run across

15

scaffolding in an abandoned mine in the dark if you'd like your services to be held with an open casket. From the garbled accounts of the one survivor, it appears they were working a tribute alone in the wee small hours when some lunatic singing to herself or simply screaming at her own demons in the dark inspired one to step off the end of a plank and the other to start down a ladder that wasn't there. They both fell over a thousand feet in the dark, and a lot of company time that could have been used to load ore had to be spent recovering the bodies, on more than one level. Our own company police searched miles of abandoned galleries in vain for the lunatic that frightened them. That's not to say she couldn't still be wandering about down there. Some of the older works from before our big consolidation six or eight years ago were never properly mapped."

Longarm smiled wearily and said, "I worked in such a mine one time when I first come West after the war. One time was enough. I'm glad I ain't been sent out here to chase haunts through played-out mine works."

"You haven't told us just what a federal deputy might *have* been sent to Virginia to do, Deputy Long," the bearded passenger said in a tone of restrained curiosity.

Longarm turned to the gal instead. "In case you're wondering, ma'am, the folks who live there call Virginia City Virginia the same way the folks who live in Dodge City call it Dodge. You just ask me all the questions about Nevada you want, and you'll find that as long as I feel free to answer 'em, I will."

Chapter 3

The grand design called for coach teams to average nine miles an hour for an hour and a half between relay stations. But since it made more sense to build stations where water was handy than it might to swap teams in the middle of nowhere, Wells Fargo had planted their Steamboat station more than halfway down from Reno, and the rest of the run took little more than a full hour. They could see the flag waving from its staff atop Mount Davidson for a good part of that hour, since the big granite dome jutted out a piece from its lesser neighbors along that reach of the eastern slope. The wagon trace took them higher along a gently graded contour line because Virginia City was a mining town and mines were sunk where you struck color. In this case at 7,200 feet above sea level, halfway up the mountain. As the trace rose, the motion-sick gal staring deperately off to the east had a view of wide-open spaces carpeted with greasewood and sage. A wide and shallow occasional stream meandering near the southern horizon was called the Carson River, named after the late Kit Carson. A silvery sheen that could have been a mirage on the horizon more to the east was called Carson Lake, and there was an even bigger sometime lake-bed called Carson's Sink sixty miles on to the northeast.

The Comstoke Lode had been found, claimed, and tunneled

into by the the first dozen or more companies in a ragged north-south line along the eroded slopes of Mount Davidson. A complex of corrugated iron roofs, tipple towers, and smoke-stacks had been allowed to just grow like Topsy, with the mine structures closest to the adits scattered across the slopes like children's discarded building blocks, until they'd gotten around to incorporating and laying out a more regular town, with streets following the north-south contour lines as straight and level as possible and named with letters from the alphabet, showing about as much imagination as they showed to name most everything else in those earlier bonanza days. The cross streets had real names and less regularity to them. Some were more like stairways. For when you built anything fronting on, say, C Street, the main business thoroughfare, your back door tended to open either underground or high in the middle of the air. Virginia City was famous for having first floors half of which were cellars in back and half of which you had to climb a flight of steps to get into from the backyards.

The houses of ill repute were mostly along D Street, where the miners could get to them without having to walk too far after work. Chinatown staggered up and down at the north end of town, where a natural spring supplied cheap, unsafe drinking water or flushed the sewage of a fair-sized town downslope to dry out in a willow tangle amid the natural greasewood and sage you'd expect to find there. The Wells Fargo coach rolled through as much of Chinatown as you could see from where the coach road turned into C Street, and then they pulled up in front of the Wells Fargo bank and stagecoach ticket office so that all but one lost soul bound for Carson City, further south, got to climb stiffly down and part friendly but fast, each to pursue his or her own sanitary facilities.

Longarm had been there before. So he toted his McClellan saddle, Winchester '73, and other baggage to the nearby Metropolitan Livery #62, and left everything but his saddlebags and rifle in their tack room.

Then he beat as much dust off himself as he could with his hat, and spent a whole dollar at the Luxor Public Baths on a barely used bar of castile soap, a clean towel, and a piping-hot tub of water nobody had ever seen before. He had to drain and refill the tub to get all the trail dirt off. He knew better than to drink any tap water while in Virginia City. A lot of folks did. Many hardrock miners held that a dash of arsenic in your drinking water was good for you. Many a sawbones made a steady living in many a mining camp treating what was known as miner's colic. Housepainters suffering lead poisoning called it painter's colic. Longarm wasn't interested in experiencing either, and he didn't care if some said he read too many books for his own good.

Once he'd wiped his saddlebags down with one end of the damp towel, Longarm changed to fresh underwear and whistled out the door, and the Paiute bath attendant brought him his beaten and brushed suit and hat along with his cleaned and polished boots. Longarm had naturally kept his gun rig and wallet to clean and dry himself. He tipped the Indian kid a whole quarter for a job well done.

Getting dressed and feeling human again, Longarm strode back to the Young America Saloon next to the livery, and bellied up to the bar in its cool armomatic depths to order a shot of Maryland Rye with a beer chaser and two bits worth of those three-for-a-nickel cheroots they had for sale on the back-bar.

His wish being their command, Longarm was nursing his beer chaser, and enjoying the smoke he'd been denying himself aboard a coach with a lady present, when another man as tall but leaner and starting to go gray at the edges joined him to quietly observe, "Figured you'd come in on the stage from Reno. I figured you'd be here or down the way at Schull & Roberts' gun store when they sent me to look for you. I'd be Senior Deputy Kevin Cole. You can call me King Cole. Everybody seems to think that's amusing and I don't really mind."

Longarm held out a hand as he replied, "I wouldn't mind being called a king either. I don't know what got into my folks when they named me Custis. I brought my own ammunition and had my guns stripped and oiled before I lit out from Denver, Your Majesty. I hope you don't think I'm drinking on duty. I figured I'd wash down some lingering trail dust and mule shit on my own time before I reported in to your boss.''

King Cole nodded and said, ''I've been sent out in the field in my time. So's my boss. The marshal says I'm to fill you in on our only reason for sending for you and then let you rip. He tells us that's what your own boss allows when the trail's gone cold and you're only playing a lukewarm tip from the keeper of a house of ill repute.''

His own boss hadn't sent him all this way without telling him why. But Longarm had been raised to be polite and nobody liked a know-it-all. So he suggested they carry a pitcher of beer over to a corner table for a sit-down discussion of the case, and King Cole agreed, seeing it had never been his own suggestion to drink on duty.

It was dark in the Young America Saloon, in contrast with the late morning sunlight outside, and there were few other customers at that hour. Few men in town without a job could afford to drink in such a middle-class establishment, and they weren't running a night shift up the slope as Consolidated picked the bones of the once-fatter Comstock Lode. A couple of old-timers were playing dominoes at a table closer to the front windows, and some volunteer firemen from the Young America hose and ladder company were nursing their beers at the bar. Longarm had discovered the Young America Saloon on an earlier visit, but hadn't gotten it straight whether the saloon was named for the fire company or vice versa. It hardly mattered as long as both outfits stayed up to scratch, and so far, Longarm hadn't noticed any just cause for a gripe.

He offered King Cole a cheroot and poured him a beer as the Virginia City District deputy began. ''You were the arresting officer over in Leadville. So we don't have to tell you what High-grade Hal Diller looks like, and you ought to be able to pick him out of the crowd of a payday night in the Crystal Palace. All we know is the son of a bitch is a middle-aged gent of average height and build and sandy coloring who may or may not have a beard or a mustache. Nobody riding with *us* has ever laid eyes on him. And worse yet, he's an experienced hardrock miner who walks like a mining man, talks like a mining man, and acts like a mining man, save for being a killer and a thief. We don't know why he came here after he busted out of Jefferson Barracks, but he has, after stabbing that federal prison guard and helping himself to civilian duds, a Schofield .45, and some traveling money by stabbing another man in Fort Leavenworth. We suspect he's committed a few other robberies at gunpoint on his way west. We know he threatened another patron of Madam Pearl's expensive parlor house after they'd both chose the same soiled dove for a French lesson. That inspired Madam Pearl to tell us he'd been staying there. The customer High-grade Hal almost cost her was a regular who spends and causes no trouble, and such customers get rarer as the Comstock Lode plays out."

Longarm blew a thoughtful smoke ring and declared, "I knew it was a mistake when Judge Dickerson sentenced Diller to life at hard instead of the rope dance. They'd told me up in Leadville that the mine foreman Diller murdered had been a good old boy for all his rough edges. But I reckon the judge was influenced by the poor cuss having some blood on his own hands, and Diller had the best lawyers hot money can buy. That madam didn't offer us any forwarding address for High-grade Hal, I take it?"

King Cole chuckled and said, "He left in a huff, owing her money, after she snapped the gun out of his hand with a wet towel. She'd made him pay in advance for his own room above the carriage house. But he'd run up a tab on food, drink, and other whorehouse favors. So he never came back for that Schofield. Lord knows what he's packing now."

Longarm sipped some suds as he considered that. "Likely another Schofield. Smith & Wesson made enough of 'em for both the U.S. Army and the Czar of All the Russians. Most cowhands prefer the cheaper and more rugged Colt '74, chambered for the same .44-40 rounds as their Winchesters. But gents such as the James boys prefer the Schofield .45, chambered for more powder than the army issues, because of the extra stopping power and way faster reloading time. Road agents and hired guns don't do as much rifle work, and being able to throw three or four times as much lead in a bank lobby or express car can add years to a gunslick's life. You've naturally asked around at all the gun shops in town, right?''

The expression on King Cole's face told him they hadn't. Longarm was too polite to comment, but King Cole asked defensively, ''What were we to ask of any gunsmith? None of us know what the son of a bitch looks like! Would you have us canvas all the outlets in a town this size by saying, 'Howdy, we're looking for an average man dressed the same as most everyone else in town who might or might not have bought a gun of any description in this place with guns for sale'?''

Longarm shrugged. ''You have to start somewhere. I take it this Madam Pearl's place would be down on D Street?''

King Cole nodded. ''South of the adit and hoist of the old Majestic Mining Company. We asked if perchance he'd had a recent photograph taken of him and that French-loving gal he'd seemed so fond of. It's surprising how many riders of the owlhoot trail have left photographic negatives scattered after them for the edification of the law. So it was worth a try. But Diller was too slick, or mayhaps he never really loved her.''

Longarm said he'd see if the outlaw they were hunting might have doubled back on his trail for another French lesson. ''Really smart gents seldom take up a life of crime to begin with, and I'm sure glad about that. Lord knows how we'd ever catch a crook who had the brains to rob just one bank and then retire to a chicken farm out California way.''

King Cole shook his head and said, ''You won't catch up with him around Madam Pearl's. Not alive leastways. I told you Madam Pearl was pissed at him.''

Longarm cocked one brow. ''A killer who'd carve his way out of a federal prison with a handmade knife would fear a female running a whorehouse?''

The local federal man nodded soberly and replied, "He would if she was Madam Pearl. All six feet and two hundred pounds of her. It wasn't a federal offense, so it ain't too clear how she settled with the State of Nevada the time she broke another surly customer's back with her own bare hands. I told you she disarmed High-grade Hal and sent him packing. Since then she's spread the word this town won't hold the two of them alive. She's probably bluffing about stalking him along C Street in broad daylight. But those who know her say they wouldn't put it past her to send for outside help that can enter all-male establishments with their own guns. So we may be doing High-grade Hal a favor by picking him up first."

Longarm blew smoke out both nostrils and decided, "Six of one and half a dozen of the other. He's never going to get off with life at hard after killing that federal guard."

A sudden thought hit him and he brightened. "I just met up with a well-known gun for hire aboard the stage from Reno. I had to put him off because he was showing off in front of a lady and making her feel anxious. You don't suppose . . ."

King Cole made Longarm tell him the whole story before he swilled some suds and declared, "I'd know Jeff Otis on sight. Do you want us to pick him up when and if he staggers into town?"

To which Longarm could only reply, "On what charge? It's likely he was on his way here to do something ferocious to somebody. But I don't see how we could prove that in any court. It would be a bother to gather the witnesses to the silly argument we had out along the wagon trace. I could be countercharged with menacing him, if his lawyers were worth their salt. The whole affair could have been dismissed as kid stuff had we not been grown men packing side arms. You've been packing a badge long as me, King Cole. You surely know the childish ways of such hairpins. Whatever he was doing aboard that stage, he started up with me for no sensible reasons I've been able to fathom."

King Cole frowned thoughtfully and said, "If Jeff Otis started up with you he had a reason. Like I said, so far he's never stepped over the federal line into our jurisdiction. But he's killed his men and gotten away with it.''

Longarm grimaced and said, ''I know. I heard about that Chinese he gunned aboard the U.P. flyer up Montana way.''

King Cole shook his head. ''You ain't been keeping score. That Chinese was ancient history. Since then he's gunned a Dutchman up in Reno and two plain Americans in Carson and Gold Hill. He set up all three the same way. Got into public arguments with them where witnesses could back his argument that he'd said he didn't want to fight. Did that more than twice in the case of that mining man in Gold Hill. Made it seem justified to the judge and jury after he felt compelled to draw in self-defense on a man who had him down as some sort of a harmless blowhard.''

Longarm said, ''Thanks for telling me. I *did* have him down as some sort of harmless blowhard, and you know what they say about once warned being thrice armed. But why in thunder would anyone send Jeff Otis after this child? I ain't done anyone in Virginia wrong so far.''

King Cole suggested, ''Maybe somebody suspects you mean to. Or hell, maybe Jeff Otis just wants to be able to brag on gunning somebody as famous as yourself. This job would be easier if men like Otis made a lick of sense.''

Chapter 4

King Cole headed back to his office, and Longarm got a room in the cleverly named Taylor Hotel at the intersection of C and Taylor Streets. He hired a corner room on the top floor, and spent a few minutes orienting himself to the lay of the land from on high.

Once you were in the city halfway up Mount Davidson, you couldn't make out the flagstaff atop the rounded-off crest. As a matter of fact, it looked more as if you were surrounded by modest hills instead of the eastern slope of a serious mountain. C Street out front ran as straight and level as anything got in Virginia City, with Taylor crossing it at an angle just right for bobsledding after a good snow. So staring east over the roof-tops in that direction to the far horizon many a desert mile off, you could tell you were a good ways above all those sage and salt flats. But when you looked around at the closer ravages of man and nature, it just seemed mighty bumpy. Any trees that had ever grown on Mount Davidson had long since gone for mine timbers or firewood, and this late in the summer the slopes were covered with grass the color of a doormat where they weren't raw sunbaked dirt and rocks. A confusion of terraced earthworks and piles of mine tailings had been spread across the original drainage contours to confuse both the eyes and the drainage. The tin roofs and false fronts along B Street, at a higher level, screened a lot of A Street and anything going on at the somewhat higher service roads beyond. So barnlike mine works, both in use and abandoned by the overall Virginia Consolidated Mining Company, stood at what seemed crazy angles from Longarm's side window. It wasn't clear whether what seemed like a railroad trestle playing peekaboo behind higher structures and smokestacks might be disconnected ore conveyors or that famous Hereford lumber flume that delivered water, firewood, and mine timbers from the higher Washoe Valley fifteen miles to the west. If it was, Longarm had read what Reporter Ramsdell of the *New York Tribune* had written about riding down it with a couple of mine owners back in '75. The article had been a grand example of the bullshit Eastern reporters kept writing about the West.

Longarm had left school early to attend a war they were having, but he could still read, write, and handle simple sums. So he didn't think much of either Reporter Ramsdell's figures or the editors who'd run his fish story in their paper without even counting on their fool fingers.

Ramsdell had reported he'd been lured to almost certain death by the mining moguls Fair and Flood, who'd assured him they often rode the flume down to Virginia to save time. Longarm was willing to buy that. But then, according to the tenderfoot at the mercy of such ruffians, the three of them had set off in a sort of pig trough shaped to fit the V-shaped flume, meaning a vessel knocked together for the trip by somebody who knew his onions. Then the next thing the poor dude knew, they were tear-assing between boulders and across canyons at a speed of a hundred miles an hour, with Ramsdell reporting, "Mountains passed like visions and shadows!" until the tenderfoot and his Wild West fellow travelers somehow made it down to Virginia City alive after tear-assing fifteen miles in just over half an hour. Reporter Ramsdell had apparently never ridden West aboard any railroad trains.

What beat all was the many times the same story had been reprinted as gospel with the figures there for any man to tally. A fifteen-mile trip would have taken fifteen minutes at sixty miles an hour, or one mile a minute. So they couldn't have averaged as much as a full thirty miles an hour, taking more than twice fifteen minutes to cover fifteen miles. But there it was in black and white, even though close to thirty miles an hour likely seemed faster in a canoe atop a trestle than from aboard a railroad car. Longarm was always winning bar bets about things reporters put in the papers when the news was slow. It was a thundering wonder how most any cuss with a vivid imagination could convince some reporter he was the lost Dauphin of France or the junior officer who'd told George Armstrong Custer not to leave those Gatling guns behind.

Thinking about vivid imaginations reminded Longarm that he didn't have all day to plan his evening in a strange town far from his usual off-duty haunts. So he draped his saddlebags over the foot of the brass bedstead, leaned the Winchester in a closet corner, and stepped outside before he shoved a match stem under the outside bottom hinge of his hall door and he locked up. Then he traipsed over to the Western Union near Wells Fargo to wire Billy Vail a progress report.

He sent it at night-letter rates to save needless expense to the taxpayers until he had something serious to report. Billy Vail had known the first moves he might make out this way before Longarm had lit out from Denver. Billy Vail had *ordered* him to just keep moving around and asking questions until he got a line on High-grade Hal Diller. A man on the run tended to keep running until he found a safe place to lay low. If that had really been Diller at Madam Pearl's, he'd been hiding out dumb as hell. Whorehouses, opium dens, and saloons, in that order, were where lawmen expected to find men on the run.

So knowing the fugitive might turn up most anywhere in Virginia, if he hadn't left town entirely after that dustup with a six-foot whore, Longarm ambled over to Piper's Opera House, built on the site of the earlier and smaller Maguire's Opera House Mark Twain had reported on, to see if Miss Roxanne Tremont, who had said she was a famous opera singer, had ever landed that job in the chorus of *The Barber of Seville*.

For if she had, and if she still admired him as much, she'd been one hell of a lay and he didn't know another friendly gal in town that summer.

He picked up some flowers along the way. Some blue chickory had sprouted in a vacant lot beween his hotel and the opera house. So he was holding them when he sashayed around to the stage door, which was open to the alley for air that afternoon. They didn't hold matinee performances in a serious working town, and the box office out front wasn't open for the evening yet. So Longarm knew that soprano trilling fit to bust somewhere inside was just practicing. Roxanne Tremont had assured him, after a swell blow job, that she had to exercise her throat muscles every day to keep them in shape.

The elderly doorman seated in a rocker with a sawed-off Greener ten-gauge knew Longarm from that earlier time when he'd been touring with the Divine Sarah Bernhardt's outfit at the behest of the U.S. State Department in order to bodyguard a treasure of France on her first American tour. So he and the doorman got along well, and Longarm was just as glad. A Greener ten-gauge was a sobering weapon to be guarding a stage door with. But the doorman was old and skinny, and some of the locals he had to deal with could be persistent when liquored up, so what the hell.

The old-timer recalled Roxanne Tremont fondly. Roxanne had that effect on men whether she went to bed with them or just allowed that some day she might. But the road company of *The Barber of Seville* had gone on to play Carson City. So there went Longarm's plans for the evening.

But just as he was looking about for trash can to toss the flowers in, two gals came out the stage door, remarking to the old man in the rocker that they were off for some tea and scones. That was what you called biscuits when you got to hanging around opera houses. Scones.

As Longarm stood there admiring the two of them, as most men would have, the more familiar-looking brunette smiled up at him, blushed, and demurely said, "Oh, Custis! You shouldn't have!"

But she took the chickory nosegay anyhow, as Longarm realized she was that gal who'd been so motion-sick and dusty aboard the stage that very morning. She introduced her auburn-haired chum as Miss Flora Livingston, and identified him as that deputy marshal she'd been talking about. Longarm still had no idea what *her* name might be. But it would have been rude to tell her he'd picked those flowers for another gal entirely.

He said he knew a swell place to order some tea and scones, but the gal who'd seemed so downcast aboard the coach that morning trilled at him not to be so forward, and suggested he take them both out for a bite after the evening performance, if he hadn't found anyone else to buy flowers, books, or candy for by then.

So Longarm just ticked his hat brim to the both of them, and they lit out with the brunette holding that clump of blue blossoms the way a Cheyenne might ride into camp with a fresh scalp.

Turning to the old doorman, Longarm smiled wearily and said, "At least she said she'd settle for flowers, books, *or* candy. A man could go broke buying all three on this child's salary. I didn't get the young lady's name just now."

The older man said, "FitzRoy. Lili FitzRoy. But she's American in spite of her French-Irish stage name. That's how come she speaks such natural English. She sings alto despite her small figure. How come I'm telling you all this? Didn't she just now tell Miss Livingston the two of you was old pals?"

Longarm said, "Some gals like to feel admired. I never paid any money for those flowers, the gal I picked 'em for ain't here, and what can it hurt if she shows off a tad to that other gal?"

He got out his pocket watch, saw it was going on four, and allowed he might or might not be back for the evening performance. He never asked what opera they might be putting on. He'd only been *acting* like a gent.

Meanwhile, the two opera gals were headed the other way, gushing like the schoolgirls they might have been if gals even younger, from working-class families, hadn't been expected to either get married up or go out and find a damned job.

Neither was aware of the two cowhands who'd ridden into Virginia with their boss on a shopping expedition. Neither cowhand had the nerve to start up with such ladies of quality, nor the desire to admire anything else within sight along the walk. So they just tagged behind, close enough to listen in and hoping one beauty or the other would say something dirty.

It was Flora Livingston who said, "When you told us about having to be saved from that brute aboard the stagecoach this morning, you never told us the swain who came to your rescue was so handsome, or that the two of you had become romantic as well!"

Lili FitzRoy modestly replied, "I'd hardly call it a romance at this stage, dear heart. I swear I gave him no encouragement. But as you just saw, he seems to feel some . . . bond between us after the danger we both shared out in the desert."

Flora sighed and said, "Some girls have all the luck. I wish I could inspire men to fight duels over me with six-shooters. So far, the best I've ever managed have never gotten past fistfights. Did that handsome thing really threaten to shoot that notorious gunman if he wouldn't leave you alone?"

Lili smugly replied, "I told you he did, didn't I? I confess I didn't know what a close call I'd had until we reached town and I was able to ask questions while I claimed my baggage. At the time I had no idea the notorious Jeff Otis was out to imperil my virtue. I had him down as simply a lecherous fellow traveler. You can imagine my surprise when I discovered I'd not only been approached by a known killer, but saved from his advances by the famous lawman they call Longarm! I heard them calling him that aboard the coach. But I didn't know how justly feared he was until he backed that sinister

Jeff Otis down and left him by the side of the trail to walk off his bad manners!''

The four of them were passing the bat-wing doors of a saloon just then. The older and wiser of the two cowhands hauled his sidekick in off the walk, saying, ''That tears it for this child.''

His pard asked plaintively, ''How come? Them townie gals were purdy as all get-out and you could tell they were both single!''

His mentor hauled him toward the bar as he growled, ''No, they ain't. They may not be married up, but you just heard the darker one confess two serious gunfighters were after her sweet ass!''

As the beefy, balding barkeep moved their way to take their orders, the younger and sillier-looking hand said, ''Shoot, I can act serious as anything with this here Remington Repeater, and I really want that little dark one!''

His pard insisted, ''No, you don't. You just heard her say she has a couple of other gents at feud for her favors. Jeff Otis is a badman from Reno you don't want to mess with, and we just heard the little lady say the other one backed Jeff Otis down! I've heard of a gun called Longarm. There ain't an ass on any mortal woman that would be worth a brush with a man who could back Jeff Otis down!''

The barkeep nodded as he waited to take their orders. A man got tired of repeating the same gossip about layoffs and banshees wailing through the deserted galleries of the worked-out Comstock Lode. So the natural gossip behind the bar could hardly wait to tell the evening regulars about a showdown brewing between two famous gunfighters in Virginia.

Chapter 5

Fancy addresses weren't up or down the slope in Virginia City. They lay toward the south, into the prevailing summer winds that followed the contours of Mount Davidson and picked up dust and less delicate odors and debris from the mine tips, stables, and pitprivvies of many a less refined address to add some interesting overtones to the sandalwood josh sticks and exotic cooking of Chinatown at the north end of town.

So Madam Pearl's would have been even farther north of the main business district if the more refined ladies in town had had anything to say about it. But since the more refined gents of town didn't care to share gals with unwashed mine hands, the most refined whorehouse in town occupied the mansion of a mining mogul who'd gone bust in the crash of '69 after he'd built in brick near the north end of D Street. The place had a nicely kept garden inside its white picket fence as well. The only evidence it might not be a one-family residence consisted of eight or ten ponies hitched out front to an unusual number of cast-iron colored stable grooms.

Longarm had arrived on foot, Virginia not being that big a town and his salary not being large enough to squander on needless livery charges. A couple of middle-aged ladies coming along the walk under parasols gave him a snooty look as he paused to let them pass before he opened the front gate.

He resisted the impulse to assure them he didn't pay for pussy. They might have taken that as a forward remark.

He mounted the steps and before he could twist the doorbell, the big front door, painted park-bench green with polished brass hardware, swung open and a pretty little thing of the African persuasion, dressed in a maid's uniform, told him gently but firmly to come back after sundown because the young ladies of the establishment were fixing to partake of their afternoon baths and a sit-down supper before the evening fun began.

Longarm smiled gently but firmly down at her and said, "I heard tell this was a high-toned establishment. But I ain't here as a customer. I am the law. U.S. Deputy Marshal Custis Long on official business. So you can invite me into your parlor and tell Madam Pearl I'm here, or I can come back with a warrant and such backup as I may require to get past such a ferocious little gal, no offense."

The maid laughed easily and told him to come on in, explaining that they'd been expecting him. She led him along a hall and up a flight of red-carpeted stairs as she explained that the madam had said to bring him right up to her as soon as he arrived.

The wood paneling all around smelled of lemon oil and French perfume. It was said a good many regulars spent over a hundred a night in such fancy surroundings. So how could an escaped federal prisoner on the run have come by the wherewithal to stay in such a place around the clock until his luck ran out?

That was one of the questions he meant to ask the old bawd who ran the fancy whorehouse. He was expecting to be led to some sort of an office. The madams and professors who kept the business ledgers of any well-run profit-making enterprise tended to be more sedate than their painted and perfumed wares.

So Longarm was surprised, but managed not to show it, when the maid led him into fancy quarters with maroon and

34

black flocked wallpaper and genuine Belgian oriental rugs to the rear of the mansion.

A big French copper bathtub with a high backrest stood in the back bay window, offering a wide view to the east and vice versa in broad-ass daylight as a big old bare-ass gal with her blond hair pinned high wallowed nipple-deep in perfumed suds.

Her broad bare shoulders were as wide as most men's, but looked mighty female. Her face wasn't bad either. She looked about the same age as him, give or take some hard living. He knew she was enjoying her soggy surprise on a man who'd been led to expect someone who looked as mean and tough as she was reputed to be.

Longarm took off his hat. Madam Pearl invited him to sit by her side on a bitty chair cushioned with red velvet to look like a big squashed tomato. When he sat he could smell her better. The undercurrent of wet female mixed with the scent of lavender bath salts made a man wish he could meet a gal like her in some other line of work.

She said, "I heard our federal gents had sent for heavy artillery. Do you boys really think Hal Diller's that dangerous? I took his gun away and threw him out downstairs all by my little old self!"

Longarm was too polite to remark on how little she might be despite her tempting smell as he modestly replied, "I wasn't sent here because of High-grade Hal's rep, Madam Pearl. It's the vague way he describes that worries your own district court. You know him on sight. I know him on sight. If you'll study on that, you'll see how tough it would be to describe him to anyone who's never laid eyes on him."

The big naked blonde nodded thoughtfully and said, "I've been over all that with Deputy Cole and the town marshal. I know none of you lawmen buy anything a woman of my social standing might say, but none of us knew he was an outlaw until after I'd chased him out in a moment of blissful ignorance. It was the other customer he'd threatened who said he was a notorious high-grader with a rep for settling arguments with a gun. Me and my young ladies had him down as a big spender in the mining game. He talked like a mining man and spent like a mining man in bonanza. Told his favorite companion, Miss Joyce, he'd just sold his claim down Arizona way to a bigger mining outfit. Said he'd come up to Virginia in hopes of prospecting for new color outside the Comstock Lode. Said he wanted to rest up and make up for some lonesome nights on the desert with his donkey before he went poking about up the slope a piece. We had no call to doubt him. Like I said, he seemed a natural mining man on a winning streak.''

Longarm nodded and said, ''That's doubtless why he likes to hang out in mining towns instead of cow towns or factory towns. What can you tell me about the customer he tangled with downstairs?''

Madam Pearl met his eyes with a level gaze of her own as she told him, ''Not much. He's a regular. He's married. We've never had trouble with him before, and I'd like to keep him as a customer. So ask no more questions about him and I'll tell you no lies about him.''

Longarm shook his head and said, ''You've already told me it was him as recognized High-grade Hal Diller for what he was. So I have to ask him where and when they'd tangled before.''

The big blonde sat up straighter, whether unaware her nipples were showing now, or wanting them to show. They sure showed perky as she insisted, ''Hell, they were only arguing about Miss Joyce, both so drunk they needed her unique services to get hard. We just agreed the both of them were mining men in a mining town. Don't ask me where they might have met before!''

Longarm insisted, ''I ain't asking *you*, ma'am. I aim to ask *him*. When you describe a gent such as High-grade Hal as a mining man, it's sort of like describing Billy the Kid as a cowboy. The last time I arrested him over to Leadville he was living up to his descriptive handle, high-grading native silver from Tabor's famous chrysolite seam. So I might find it fruitful to compare notes with another gent who might have a better grasp on what might attract a high-grader to the almost-played-out Comstock Lode.''

She replied, ''Hand me that Turkish towel behind you, will you?'' as Longarm realized for the first time that maid had crawfished out of the room to leave just the two of them to sort things out between them.

Longarm had to rise to reach the towel draped over the back of yet another chair. When he turned, he saw Madam Pearl had risen like Venus from the waves in that famous Italian painting. Only the naked gal in the painting had some long hair hiding her privates, while all of *this* naked gal's hair was pinned atop her head. And there was sure a lot more of her standing there, all wet, soap-slicked, and as casual as if he'd been that colored maid.

Longarm moved over to just hand the fool towel to her. He'd noticed traveling with the Divine Sarah and some other road shows in his time, that gals who changed duds a lot under crowded conditions didn't seem to care who saw their bare tits and lap fuzz as long as they didn't get in the way. Men who worked behind the scenery in opera houses or whore-houses had to just go on about their business in front of gals in all states of *dishabille*. That was what the Divine Sarah had called it when she ran all around backstage with her duds half on or all the way off—*dishabille*.

It would have been rude to sit back down while a lady was standing tall and drying her tits and ass off. So Longarm went on standing, hat in hand, as he said, ''You were about to tell me where that other man who knew High-grade Hal on sight might be found, Madam Pearl.''

She said, ''No, I wasn't. Those stories about me charging a thousand dollars for my own personal services are not true. I haven't had to put out for cash since I charged *more* than a thousand a pop, during the last wild trading in mining stocks, and bought this place to make money the easy way with the sweat of *other* brows.''

Longarm refrained from asking how her gals wound up with

sweat on their foreheads, and insisted, "I can find out from others who you're trying to shield from me, ma'am. Once I do, I'll be calling on him where he lives, and didn't I just hear you say he was a married man?"

She stepped out of the tub to move closer, stark naked and so long of limb he'd only have to whip it out and shove it in. But when she put her free hand to his belt buckle, Longarm gently but firmly grasped her wrist and insisted, "That ain't what I came here to ask of you, ma'am."

She laughed. "What's the matter? Don't you like girls?"

To which he could only reply, "More than words can say, and later tonight I'm surely going to cuss myself and my boss a heap. But like I said, that ain't what I'm asking!"

She sighed. "Let me tell him you want to talk to him and we'll see if he's willing. As a man of the world you surely know how long I'd stay in business if word got out that anything a gentleman might want to do or say within these walls wasn't as confidential as the confessions of a sinner to his parish priest!"

Longarm allowed he could keep a secret once he gave his word to do so. So she asked him to dry her back, and he did. She was sort of soft for such a big strapping gal. But her wide hips and ample cheeks were solid enough. When she bent over to grasp the rim of the tub and asked him to dry the crack of her ass, he said he'd rather not.

She took the towel from him to grasp at both ends and dry her own crotch with enthusiasm as she told him, "You're no fun. I haven't been laid for over a month. Not because I'm too shy but because I'm particular. Why don't you take off your own clothes so we can both get out of this ridiculous vertical position, Longarm? It's not as if I've never heard of you and your *own* wicked ways, you know. Why else would I have invited you up here while I was in this state of undress?"

Longarm said, "To see if you could keep me from pestering that gent who could identify a federal want on sight. I'm sorry if things you've heard about this child led you to believe he was a total chump a nice-looking gal could lead down the primrose path by his pecker. But you heard wrong, Madam Pearl. I'd be a liar if I said I didn't want you so bad right now I can taste it. I'd be a bigger liar if I intimated I ain't played slap and tickle with uglier gals who could have used all that soap and water you just climbed out of. But what I do on my own time for innocent merriment is one thing, and what I do when I'm on the trail of a wanted killer is another. So when will you know whether that other gent's willing to talk to me or not?''

She said, "Come back around midnight. I'll have him wait for you after he's relaxed with Miss Joyce. Provided he comes in and providing he's willing.''

Longarm said, "Make sure he does and he is, unless you want me to do it the hard way. That argument he had with Diller in your taproom wasn't half as private as the average church confession booth. So why don't you remind him of that and see if we can't keep the whole thing friendly and discreet.''

She said she'd try. Then she dropped her towel to wrap both big arms around him and plaster her naked body to the front of his tweed outfit as she kissed him warmly, wetly, and French.

He kissed her back the same way, being only human, and it seemed only polite to run his hands down her smooth bare back to steady her on her bare toes with a good grip on her mighty tempting bare ass.

But then he got out of there before it got any harder on him. For a lawman who fornicated with a potentially hostile witness before he swore out a court order on her was a lawman who deserved to be sweeping out stables with his bare feet.

That pretty colored maid let him out, looking surprised to see him leaving so early. He felt sort of surprised himself. He'd have had a tougher time breaking away from all those naked charms if they hadn't belonged to a total whore as well as a possible arrest. He told himself to forget how swell more than one such gal could screw for free just for pleasure. Screwing, like any other skill, improved as you got to practice at it. So it sort of hurt to think what a thousand-dollar-a-night professional could do for a man she really felt like screwing.

Sundown commenced early on the eastern slopes of any mountain range, and so it was going on dusk by the time Longarm had stoked his gut with roast beef, potatoes and beans, and coffee and cheescake, and headed back to his hotel.

He aimed to take his own bath and shave the day's stubble before he went back out to prowl the bright sports of C Street for his fugitive.

But as he approached his locked door with his hired key, he spotted a match stem on the hall runner where no match stem would have been if somebody hadn't opened his door and dislodged it from where he'd left it wedged under the bottom hinge.

Turning a key in a lock at such a time could take fifty years off a man's life. He put the key away and drew his .44-40. Sometimes you could just twist the knob and go on in. Other times somebody would lob a few rounds through the door to let you know for sure you'd been right about that match stem.

So Longarm stood out of the line of fire as he gingerly turned the knob, found the latch unlocked, and flung the door wide to throw down on anybody in there.

As he did so, the naked redhead who'd been reclining in his bed sat up with a weary smile, bare tits aimed back at him in the soft light of the bed lamp, and said, "Custis Long, you perambulating man! Where on earth have you been all afternoon? I was about to start without you! I have to get on over to the Crystal Palace any minute! So get out of those fool pants and prepare to take your beating like a man!"

Chapter 6

Few natural men would have needed further invitation to bolt the door and shuck their duds. For Longarm and the famous saloon piano player known to her many admirers as Red Robin had known one another, in the biblical sense, since first he'd arrested her down Texas way as a murder suspect.

Red Robin threw the covers aside as he joined her on the bedstead, and Longarm was delighted as ever by how different two naked ladies could be without either of them being ugly.

The naked redhead would have barely come to the big blonde Madam Pearl's bare shoulder, and wasn't as wide across the hips, although Red Robin was built fleshy enough and her tits stuck out as far. Longarm had resisted Madam Pearl's invitation as she'd stood there with a shaved snatch. Red Robin shaved her snatch too—for sanitary reasons, as she said, or maybe to hide the fact that she wasn't a natural redhead from her closer friends.

Unlike that big bold blonde, the short frisky redhead had been wed a time or more, but never sold her intimate favors for money, proving the exception to the rule that practice made perfect. For despite all the lessons and practice, Red Robin had never learned to play the piano half as well as she could screw.

So Longarm screwed her, and then some, as she did her

best to buck him out of her soft compact love-saddle without letting go of his old organ-grinder with her tight throbbing innards.

They came together fast, for practice, and settled down to a nice long lope to Paradise and back with both pillows under her rolicking rump and Longarm's bare feet against the brass rails at the foot of the bedspread for purchase as the two of them made the springs squeal like a litter of piglets under them. She laughed like a dirty little kid, and asked him to feel her winking rectum when she felt his love juices overflowing and running down the crack of her ass. He obliged her with two fingers in her slippery back entrance as she tried to swallow him, balls and all, up front with her shapely legs, sheathed in black mesh, spread wider than most gals could manage.

But all good things had to end, and the two of them finally had to pause for a cuddle and a smoke as they fought to get their breathing under control. As Longarm fumbled for the vest he'd dropped somewhere to fish out the required cheroot and matches, Red Robin held on to his semi-erection with one fond piano-playing hand and murmured, "I'm going to be late at the Crystal Palace, but fuck 'em. They can wait. I only came to warn you, but when they said you were out and I got them to let me wait for you up here, this bed was just too tempting, and aren't you glad I have such a weak nature, Custis?"

Longarm rolled closer with the fixings and put one arm around Red Robin's creamy shoulders to snuggle her head on his own as he thumbnailed a light and got their one cheroot going. As she started to play with his pecker, he said, "You're going to show up for work even later if you arouse that sleeping monster. What was it you came to warn me about so sweetly, kitten?"

Red Robin said, "I'm not a kitten. I'm a hungry little bird who can't seem to get her fill of this big fat worm. As I just told you, I've been engaged to entertain at the Crystal Palace near the opera house. I play some sets for a noonday crowd and two or three more for the more serious drinking and gambling after sundown. So this afternoon I heard you were in town, which thrilled my soul. Then I heard a famous gunslick had limped in from the north all hot and dusty, swearing he meant to clean your plow, and this inspired me to scout around to see where you might be staying and tell you he was after you. All I managed to overhear for certain was that he hailed from Reno and answered to the name of Otis.''

Longarm place the cheroot between her lush lips as he soothingly said, ''Jeff Otis. Don't worry your pretty little head about him. I did have words with him earlier today, and he'd be the first to tell you how rough and ready he might be. But he reads as a blowhard with a string of unfair fights to his brag.''

Red Robin handed the cheroot back and tried to drop a smoke ring around the head of the pecker she was stroking before she declared, ''The sweet man who carries this wonder around could lie just as limp and dead after an *unfair* fight as he could any other kind. The customer who brought the news to the Crystal Palace this afternoon *said* Otis had gunned somebody dirty over in Gold Hill.''

Longarm explained, ''He pled self-defense to get off too. I've met up with his breed before. You have to watch 'em. But they seldom have the nerve to either draw on you or shoot you outright in the back. The cuss is a gun for hire who likes to advertise. Just *saying* he's at feud with another reputed quick-draw man is as likely to impress his public as a real showdown might. You've doubtless heard the different versions of that famous showdown betwixt Wild Bill and John Wesley Hardin. I've never got it clear in my mind whether Hardin was gunning for James Butler Hickok in Abilene or vice versa. They both had half the folks in town braced for a dreadful shootout that just never took place, whilst it enhanced the reps of both as serious gunfighters. Old Hickok and the Thompson brothers added to their reps in Abilene with a heap of tough talk too. But the only famous gunfighter Hickok ever had to shoot in Abilene was Phil Coe.''

Longarm took a drag on the cheroot and added, ''Phil Coe was a famous gunfighter after Hickok shot him. Up until that time his most famous offense against law and order was a saloon sign deemed obscene by the ladies of Abilene.''

Red Robin gave his pecker a playful jerk and confided, "I heard about that sign in front of the Bull's Head Tavern in Abilene. The bull on the sign had one of *these* obscene things hanging down to the ground, right?''

Longarm said, "So I've heard. Phil Coe and Ben Thompson both had interests in the Bull's Head Tavern. When Marshal Hickok showed up with a ladder and a bucket of paint to turn that bull into a steer nobody found as offensive, Ben Thompson had the sense to back off. Phil Coe got likkered up and spent the next twenty-four hours bragging on what he meant to do to Wild Bill Hickok, the bastard. Then he compounded his foolishness by firing wild shots outside the Alamo Saloon till Hickok came outside armed and dangerous. Coe still might have saved his fool self. Hickok held his fire when the drunk allowed he'd only been shooting at a stray hound. But then he pegged two more wild bragging shots in Hickok's general direction, and died along with an innocent bystander in their lines of fire. You have to know what you're doing when you get to bragging with guns. Every now and again somebody really gets shot. Poor old Hickok was gunned five years after he gunned Coe and that bystander, his own pal Deputy Mike Williams.''

Red Robin asked if a French lesson might get it all the way up for her again, adding, "I really do have to get my ass over to the Crystal Palace ere long, lover.''

Longarm snuffed out his cheroot to kiss her and feel her up right before he turned her over on her hands and knees to enter her doggy-style with renewed interest and both feet on the rug.

Holding a well-padded hip in each palm, Longarm was able to talk while he worked in that position, which was likely why it was such a popular position with old pals.

As she arched her spine to take it deeper, Longarm said, "I'll run you over to your job any minute now. You forgot to explain why you're entertaining here in Virginia, Miss Red Robin. No offense, but we've met more often in mining camps where they were enjoying boom times with the color and day wages flowing free. Last I heard about that Comstock Lode up the slope, the big combination mining what was left of low-grade ore scientifically had cut salaries and laid off half the miners on the one shift a day they're still using.''

Red Robin lowered her unpinned red mop to the mattress and said, ''Faster, faster, I really have to get back to work. As to how come I was hired to entertain at the fanciest saloon in town, there's still over a thousand gents all told working for Consolidated Virginia, and we tend to get the ones on higher wages at the Crystal Palace. I got to play for some other entertainers touring with *The Barber of Seville* a while back, and there's other fresh money coming in attracted by tales of fresh strikes on the mountain!''

Longarm thrust all the way in and rubbed the head of it around on her slippery cervix as he frowned thoughtfully and replied, ''Do tell? It's a good-sized mountain, but it ain't as if nobody's looked anywhere else for outcrops in the nearly twenty years since O'Riley and McLaughlin first panned color in what was once upon a time a mountain spring named for Old Man Caldwell. Lord knows *where* that spring springs now. It's doubtless just as well. Virginia's earlier drinking water assayed considerable gold, silver, and arsenic and . . . hold on, I'm fixing to come some more!''

That made two of them. Red Robin told him not to take it out to turn her over, but just pound her down through the bedsprings as she moaned and clawed the bottom sheet in sheer delight.

But once more they had to stop when they'd run out of steam, and they were both experienced enough at the game to know it was better to get washed up and dressed while they were still out of breath than to have to quit while they felt able.

Longarm let Red Robin at the corner washstand first, knowing it took gals longer to fix their hair and powder their noses after a whore bath. As he soaped and rinsed his own privates at the stand, while Red Robin put herself back together for the evening, he repeated what he'd said about the Comstock Lode's future potential.

She said she'd heard a smaller outfit had filed a new claim higher on the mountain after somebody pulling stumps for firewood had found blossom rock clinging to some roots, or vice versa. Longarm whistled thoughtfully and declared, "You find blossom rock as a sort of bacon rind wrapped around serious color-bearing quartz. So what they think they've struck depends a heap on how far from the main Comstock Lode they've struck it."

She said she didn't get his drift as she pinned her henna-red hair. Gals sure looked nice when they had their bare arms up like that, with some chest still showing above the bodice of a red velvet piano-playing dress. Red Robin seemed to think that color favored her.

Longarm dried his crotch as he explained, "If somebody dug into an outcrop of blossom rock within a furlong of the main lode, it would only mean some sort of leftover crust. If they'd hit color more than, say, a quarter mile clear of the already explored blue quartz under this slope, it could mean a whole new mother lode! Bigger, smaller, the same size, and still a wonder to be jawed about on Wall Street. For they sure got a heap of bullion out of this mountain so far, and you just don't find much blossom rock any distance from the more solid quartz you have to rot with groundwater for a few million years to get that soft!"

Red Robin brightened and said, "Oh, you mean this blossom rock they keep talking about is a sort of *indication* of greater riches to come?"

Longarm bent to pick up his shirt as he replied, "That's about the size of her. Blossom rock tends to be richer in color than the mother lode it crumbled away from. The groundwater carries away a lot of the salts and silicates to leave more metal behind. But after that, like I said, it's just a sort of crust. Worth working by shovel and pan, of course. But bottoming out to either serious ore or plain old country rock, depending on which way you're digging."

Red Robin confessed she knew more about music than mining, and asked what Longarm had come to Virginia for, aside from what he'd just done to her.

Longarm hauled on his pants as he said she'd just told him, adding, "I'm here to give other lawmen a hand with a fugitive I know on sight. I've been wondering what a crook known for high-grading could be up to around a low-grade operation. But now that you've mentioned a new strike in blossom rock, I suspect High-grade Hal Diller must have heard the same rumors."

He explained high-grading as he walked her after dark to the Crystal Palace. Or he tried to. Red Robin had worked enough mining camps to have picked up some mining lore without having to study on it. Hence she'd already heard about miners who went into business on their own with a pocketful or a carload of selected samples from bulk ore on its way to the mill.

The Crystal Palace wasn't made out of crystal. It had been named for the more famous Crystal Palace in London's Regent's Park. But it was just a fancier than usual saloon with the bar and gaming tables on the main floor and more delicate surroundings on the top gallery wrapped around and overlooking the cruder crowd below. Red Robin played piano near one end of the bar on the main floor. Longarm let go of her arm and entered a couple of paces behind her, looking as if butter wouldn't melt in his mouth when the night manager thundered over to ask where in blue blazes she'd been all this time.

Red Robin allowed she'd been in Heaven, and offered to go back up and play for the angels if he didn't like it. Longarm moved toward the bar as Red Robin flounced on to the piano amid thunderous applause.

Longarm had told Red Robin he had to go back to that whorehouse at midnight on official business. So she'd said to make sure it remained official business, and given him her room number at her own hotel in case he didn't feel sleepy when she got off around one A.M.

47

So he was nursing a stein at the bar while Red Robin played "Lorena," unless it was "Aura Lee," when a waiter came to the bar with a tray of empties and told Longarm a lady with that opera party up in the gallery had invited him to join them.

Longarm hadn't known there was any sort of party up yonder under the eaves. He stepped clear of the bar to peer up through the smoke as Red Robin gave up trying to decide between "Lorena" and "Aura Lee," and started up with the easier-to-follow "Sweet Betsy from Pike." So mining boots were stamping in time with Red Robin as Longarm made out the smiling faces of both the auburn-haired Flora Livingston and the brunette Lili FitzRoy staring back down at him. The brunette who'd been so sick aboard the morning coach looked bright-eyed and raring to go. So Longarm went over to the stairs lest Red Robin notice her, or vice versa.

The petite brunette met him at the head of the stairs, while the gal he'd just laid chased Sweet Betsy and her lover, Ike, across the ivory keys. Red Robin hadn't figured out the black keys yet.

Ticking his hat brim to another woman entirely, Longarm said, "Evening, Miss Lili. I was under the impression you'd be singing alto over to the opera house about now."

The opera singer who bragged on famous lawmen saving her from roughnecks trilled, "Canceled to the end of the week. Some of our scenery is still en route from the Reno railroad yards aboard ox-drawn freight wagons. So my evenings will be free, free, free, while you show me the wonders of the West. There are some wonders around here, aren't there?"

Chapter 7

Lili dragged Longarm along the gallery to where two tables were jammed together to serve the baker's dozen from the opera company. Only four of them were gals, but the male singers were almost soft and pretty enough to make their gender uncertain. Lili made a gent she introduced as a tenor pour Longarm a tumbler of the fancy French punch they were drinking instead of needled beer. He was sorry he'd left his beer stein on the bar until he tasted the pink stuff. But soon he was just as glad. They'd spiked the red wine and lemonade to at least sixty proof.

Longarm was afraid Lili was going to go on about that kid stuff on the stage from Reno. But the topic of the conversation seemed to be the piano-playing down on the main floor. Longarm had already noticed Red Robin seemed a tad tone-deaf. But opera folks who'd studied music seriously seemed to find Red Robin's efforts grotesque. That was what the plump and pallid tenor who'd served him called Red Robin—grotesque.

The auburn-haired Flora smiled sort of dirty, and suggested a lady who played piano like that had doubtless fallen back on other talents to get the job, and everybody but Longarm laughed.

There was no delicate way he could say he knew for certain that Red Robin never fucked where she worked. It was yet

49

another opera gal, a soprano with light brown hair called Miranda, who guessed how Longarm's poker-faced reaction to the banter about the gal downstairs might read and stared his way as she declared, "I'm not so certain we should hold the unfortunate young woman to our own musical standards."

Flora simpered and said, "That hair's unfortunate, all right. I used to have a bitty wagon that same color."

This time Miranda didn't join the laugh that went round either. She said, "Oh, for heaven's sake, the poor thing's seated at an out-of-tune upright, entertaining a rather uncouth crowd in a working-class saloon. Of course she has to make herself up for the part. Would you have me sing the role of Norma without a long blond wig and my Druid robes? That other *artiste* you're being so cruel about is no doubt as aware as the rest of us of the latest fashions, and wears them, when she's not required to appear in that dreadful red velvet mess! Don't you agree, ah . . . Custis?"

Longarm nodded, although he knew that in truth Red Robin was so fond of that low-cut velveteen outfit she'd had copies made so she could dress the same way while one or more was being dry-cleaned. Red Robin was picky as hell about sanitation, considering her sort of dirty mind.

He knew all too well how Red Robin's mind was likely to read things the minute she spotted him up there sipping fancy punch with those high-toned opera gals. His conscience was clear. Wanting to kiss a gal with light brown hair didn't count as long as you kept such notions to yourself. But he knew as soon as Red Robin finished her set and spied him up there, she'd be on her way up to horn in, and while he doubted anyone was likely to wind up on her ass with a busted nose, he knew a tone-deaf country girl he'd once cleared of a murder charge wasn't going to hold still for much veiled sarcasm before she told someone sweetly to just go fuck themselves.

Meanwhile, Red Robin was doing her best to play "Abraham's Daughter," no doubt by request, and some mining men down below proceeded to stomp their boots in time as they sang, more in tune than Red Robin.

> Oh, we belong in the infantry,
> And don't you think we oughter?
> We're marching down on Richmond Town.
> To fight for Abraham's Daughter!

This had inspired another bunch at the other end of the bar to wail in counterpoint to Red Robin and the obvious Union vets about the dusky charms of the Yellow Rose of Texas, a high-yaller slave gal Sam Houston had sent to spy on General Santa Anna in his very own field cot. Such notions about faithful darkies still had a lot of former slave owners confused.

As one of the Union men broke a bottle on the zinc-topped bar at their end, Longarm caught the eye of that tenor and moved closer to mutter, "When it starts I'll try to hold the stairs. You and these other gents see if you can get the ladies out the back way, and don't stop running till you're holed up in your hotel. Any questions?"

He liked the opera singer better when the soft-looking cuss shook his head and said, "This isn't my first time on the road."

But nothing seemed to be turning out the way Longarm expected in Virginia City. For just as one of those unreconstructed rebels busted a beer stein to provide himself with a right nasty weapon, another man appeared in the doorway, fired his six-gun out the door to gain some attention, and roared, "We got that banshee cornered in the Sutro and who's coming with me to lend a damned hand?"

Half the men on the floor below stampeded for the door, that other war forgotten, as Red Robin banged out something that sounded like "The Gerry Owen."

Longarm knew he'd never get a better offer for a graceful exit, and to hell with whether the Denver District Court had jurisdiction on Irish superstitions or not. So he ticked his hat to the ladies and declared he had to join that informal *posse comitatus*. Then he ran down the stairs before anyone there could ask him what on earth he was talking about.

Out on the street, it seemed most of the milling crowd was for just running down the damned mountain on foot. Longarm grabbed a volunteer fireman with an ax to ask how far they were talking about running.

The local man said, "Sutro tunnel entrance at the bottom of the slope. Say three miles as the crow flies or three thousand feet as a turd might fall. Let go my damned arm. I could have been halfway by now!"

Longarm let him run on, and trotted to the corner after him. As soon as Longarm was on the steeply graded side street, he saw that a man in low heels could almost fly down the mountain. So he flew, knowing it would take longer to hire a livery mount, only have to tether it to something at the bottom of the slope, than it would take him to just leg on down. He'd worry about getting back up the fool mountain once he knew why he was running down it.

A legged-up infantryman could march a mile in less than a quarter hour on level ground. A trained athlete could run it in less than five minutes. Longarm was neither, but he was trotting downhill, so it wasn't too long before he was slipping and sliding through sagebrush and cheat to see torchlights massing around something in the darkness below. He heard his name being called, and saw to his surprise he was trotting on down in company with that plump tenor from the opera company. *His* name was something like Santini, Enzio Santini. Longarm called out, "This ain't your fight, no offense. Are you packing any hardware under that fresh-cleaned and pressed frock coat?"

The dude in the sort of sissy duds and white planter's hat patted his side to reply, ".445 Webley Bulldog. I told you this wasn't my first time on the road. What do these mining men mean by a banshee? The only banshee I've ever heard of was a sort of Irish evil spirit!"

Longarm jumped over some greasewood and grunted, "We've been hearing the same old country fairy tales. Nobody expects to catch a real haunt down yonder. Some crazy lady seems to be wandering around in the mines, wailing in a high soprano and scaring the shit out of everybody.''

Santini laughed incredulously and yelled, ''All this lunacy over a disturbing voice? Remind me not to leave any windows open while we're rehearsing backstage at the opera house! Some of the arias in *Norma* are rather dreadful even when sung in tune!''

A trio of hands further down the slope suddenly went down as if hit by flanking fire. Longarm warned, ''Drift fence ahead!'' and dropped to the ground to roll under the bottom strands of bobwire, tasting the dust he was getting all over his tweed outfit. He had to allow the soft-looking Santini was a sport when he rose on the far side to see that the tenor had rolled on down the mountain with him.

''Why did we just do that?'' Santini asked as they trotted on after others toward the gathering galaxy of torchlight in the distance.

Longarm explained, ''Range cows wandering into town can be a bother. They usually graze grassy slopes, and folks truck-farm the flatlands within easy driving to a fair-sized town. Watch out for cow pats down here where they've rooted out the greasewood and sewn some gramma seed. I doubt we have to worry about falling in any irrigation ditches on this side of the Sutro.''

He'd thought everybody had heard tell of the Sutro by this time, but Santini was an opera singer and had to ask.

As they trotted on down toward it, Longarm explained, ''Things up the slope got in an awful mess as the different crews mined down ever deeper at different speeds through groundwater hot, cold, and just plain nasty. There's some argument whether working half-naked with acid water dripping on you is worse than wading through alkali that dissolves your boot leather and then chaws off your feet. Pumping a shaft can only help so much as the shaft gets deeper. So a few years back this Swiss mining engineer called Adolph Sutro drove a swamping tunnel in from the baseline of the whole blamed mountain to let all the slop from the works above trickle down from above and just run out on the desert flats into settling ponds where the sun could dry it way cheaper. See?"

Santini said, "I think so. Why would even a mad soprano want to wail in a big drainage tunnel at this hour?"

To which Longarm could only reply, "I don't know. If they catch her she may tell 'em. There's this old church hymn you might not have to learn to sing in operas that's called 'Farther Along.' I'd sing her for you, but you'd just laugh. So take my word, the sense of the song is that farther along we may know more than we do right now. I have found that notion a fine way to calm my nerves when I don't know what in the hell I'm doing."

Grass and even shrubbery grew thicker now as they neared the foot of the slope and pushed through some rabbit bush and desert willow to join the torchlit mob around the concrete archway marking the entrance to the Sutro Tunnel. There was nothing in the way of a gate across the yawning black hole in the mountain. Old Sutro himself had sold his four miles of nothing bored through quartz-veined granite to the mining syndicate for enough to move on to Frisco, where when last heard from, he'd started building a monstrous Roman bath along a clifftop overlooking the Pacific and planted a whole forest of Australian trees on top of another high rise.

As they moved into better light, Longarm saw that Santini's sort of French blue coat showed more dirt than his own tobacco tweed. A man who chased others along the owlhoot trail had to plan ahead when he bought a damned suit because the Hayes Reform Administration had such a fussy civil service dress code. Longarm saw that older Gould & Curry accountant, Nat Rothfeld, jawing with a younger man wearing a pewter badge and a Remington .45, backed by a Bullard eleven-shot repeating rifle. Rothfeld had a Spencer .52 cradled over his arm, but was otherwise dressed for bookkeeping in his shirtsleeves and vest with a side-draw Manhattan .36 five-shooter.

Longarm led Santini over, and introduced him to the accountant and what turned out to be a town deputy named Howell. He asked how come all of them seemed to be standing about out there in the open air if that mysterious whatever was raising Ned inside the mountain.

Howell explained they were waiting for a senior lawman to come down the outside of the mountain. Most of the company police and a bunch of town lawmen were *inside* the mountain at higher levels, working their way down. When Howell allowed he didn't have the rank to lead anybody inside, Longarm snorted in disgust and asked, "What did they pin that to your vest for, to make sure the boys playing marbles after school never cheated? There's one hell of a tangle of tunnels, drifts, and shafts at the far end of this entrance way, old son. If all of us down here with all these torches were to take up positions all along the three miles of the riddled lode, we'd have that banshee sort of illuminated from below to the others chasing her deeper from the adits up along the top of it, see?"

Howell said he did, but added that he still didn't feel he had the authority to take charge down there.

Longarm said, "Aw, shit." Then he raised his voice to call out in the night, "I'm going in after the critter. Anybody who wants to follow me is free to do so. Anybody who ain't is free to just stand here and wave them fool torches at the moon."

Then he drew his .44-40, held out a hand for a torch, and once he had one in his left hand, headed into the Sutro, splashing some in the thin sheet of water flowing across the slick floor of tamped earth.

As he strode along what seemed at first a big sewer, lined with the same concrete over wire mesh as the entrance, he saw Nat Rothfeld and Enzio Santini were tagging along with torches of their own. Santini had drawn his ugly snub-nosed Webley, and the accountant had the muzzle of his seven-shot Spencer trained ahead into the darkness. Longarm had read how George Washington had never looked behind him as he'd led that advance at Princeton Town, lest his men suspect he wasn't sure he could count on them. But he could tell by the sounds of splashing bouncing off the cement all around, and the shadows leading the way into the unlit unknown, that he had enough company to matter, even as Nat Rothfeld was griping, "Longarm, what the hell are we doing?"

Longarm said, "Go on back and stargaze to your heart's content."

The accountant protested, "I never said I wanted to turn back. I only wanted to know the *verflucht* plan you had in mind!"

Before Longarm could answer, the blackness ahead echoed to a scream of sheer madness, wailing higher and higher until it seemed almost too high for anybody but bats to make out.

Nat Rothfeld gasped, "*Oy, Gottelyu!* What was that?"

Enzio Santini decided, "A over high C. I've never heard any human soprano hit that note before!"

Rothfeld demanded, "*Nu,* what makes you think you're hearing a human voice now?"

It was a good question. Longarm said, "Let's go find out. That's the plan you were asking about, Nat. First we catch the banshee and then we ask her if she's human or not. We sure as shit ain't about to find out any other way!"

Chapter 8

The wailing echoes died away, and Longarm led those still willing to follow him deeper into the dripping darkness. Deputy Howell was only one of those who'd bolted for the entrance to wait for the U.S. Cav or whatever. As Longarm and a score of sterner stuff moved farther along the Sutro, the damp air in the tunnel grew ever warmer. Longarm could only imagine how awful the heat under Mount Davidson had been before old Adolph Sutro punched this hole in the bottom of the boiler. It felt as if they were in the belly of some great beast by the time they'd worked their way in to where you could look up along some stretches of the Sutro into the timber boxwork that rose up and up out of torchlight reach, only to be replaced a few yards along by the dripping arched roof of the Sutro, solid timber this far under the lode, with thin streams of water pouring hot or cold through the cracks between the massive planks. Then you'd come to another mined-out furlong with some of the boxwork holding catwalks at different bewildering levels, and others just full of hot air for as high as the flickering light could reach. The miners were inclined to either fill in the fathom-square cubes with spent ore, or salvage the walkways nobody had to walk along anymore.

They came to a sort of four-square cascade where four

sheets of drainage ran down the square framework of a hoist shaft piercing the roof timbers. Longarm had no call to soak his hat and suit while he drowned his torch. So he edged around the falling sheets, closer to the tunnel wall, as others perforce formed a single file behind him.

So he'd moved beyond, holding his torch high against the blackness beyond, when all Hell broke loose right behind him!

He whirled around after the muzzle of his six-gun as crazy high-pitched wailing cut loose just as Nat Rothfeld commenced to fire .52 rifle rounds from his repeating Spencer to drown the banshee out, and then some, filling the Sutro with ear-ringing echoes and a whole lot of gunsmoke!

So Longarm wasn't sure what he was looking at, and held his fire as a dimly visible figure spun wildly and kept screaming in the center of that cube of falling water for perhaps another two seconds before it just rose up and up some more, as Santini and some others joined Nat Rothfeld's fusillade with rapid fire of their own!

Then whatever it was had risen clean out of sight, even as it wailed down the smoke-filled shaft at them. The opera tenor stepped through the falling water to fire his .445 straight up the shaft as his torch went out. Then Longarm yelled, "Hold your fire!" as he heard distant and more human voices calling back and forth at some higher level.

In the sudden silence Longarm and the men with him heard somebody else calling, "She's over yonder and, Sweet Jesus, look at her go!"

Then they heard other gunshots, loud enough to fill the whole big Consolidated mine with confusing echoes, even at that distance.

Santini bent to pick something up before he ducked out through the cascading drainage again, planter's hat and fancy duds both wet and muddy. Holding his find up to the better light of Rothfeld's torch, he said, "Papier-mâché with some glued-on hair. You hit the mask some acrobat was wearing, Mr. Rothfeld!"

The accountant said, "Oy, look at me, I'm a sharpshooter!

So how did it scamper up a waterfall after I shot it in the head with a .52-caliber rifle round? You wear a mask over your *face* as a rule. So why shouldn't there be some real flesh and blood?''

Longarm stepped closer for a better look. He saw the ''hair'' looked more like strands of gray thread. He knew cheaper theatrical wigs were made of that rather than real and expensive human hair. Horsehair just didn't hang right. He said, ''The prankster had a fake head worn over his or her own, like a hat instead of a mask. The notion was to look less logical as it bounded about in its spooky outfit. That has to be it because you're right about a regular mask having a face on the far side of it, Nat. You're pretty good with that Spencer. Where'd you learn to fire that straight that sudden?''

The accountant shrugged modestly and said, ''What can I tell you? I told them I was better with figures, but they put me on Little Round Top under Chamberlain at Gettysburg.''

To which Enzio Santini replied, ''Hey, you were on Little Round Top at Gettysburg! I was with the Iron Brigade on Cemetery Ridge!''

Some of the others who considered themselves more country laughed at the exchange. Longarm didn't. He'd been in action with ribbon clerks and dance instructors who'd made tolerable soldiers, along with many a country boy who'd cut and run. The only way to find out whether a man had grit or not was to watch which way he ran when things got gritty. Both dudes had lost the fancy accents they usually put on, but neither had turned tail, which was more than some of the more country boys in the Sutro could say by then. So Longarm beamed fondly on the baker's dozen still with him and declared, ''Those others in the boxwork high above are in a better position to chase whatever that was just now. Our best bet would be to move back to where this tunnel's roof is solid and make our own stand against Miss Banshee there, where she ain't got room to bound about like that.''

Nobody argued, and by the time they'd sloshed a few furlongs closer to fresh air, Nat Rothfeld was starting to sound more like a college graduate again when Longarm asked him to think back and describe that hasty target more exactly.

The accountant shrugged and replied, "What's to describe? I fired on sight when it dropped down from above, landed in a spidery crouch, and bounced back up screaming at me that way! I thought I'd hit it. Santini here agrees I must have grazed it at least. Then it was gone again, faster than it takes to tell. Plop, scream, poof, up the chimney he rose, she rose, or whatever that was rose!"

"But what did it *look* like?" Longarm insisted.

"Gray," said Rothfeld, and others there agreed as he went on to describe a hasty glimpse of what seemed an old gray-headed crone in a tattered gray funeral shroud. "Her face looked gray and dead, but since Santini thinks that was a mask, there's no saying *what* that screaming freak really looked like without its costume. An acrobat that agile could make a fortune touring with a circus, and he or she couldn't be that old."

Santini said, "Amen, and it was a she. Nobody with *balls* could yell, never mind sing, at such a pitch!"

Longarm was inclined to read at random from the stacks of the Denver Public Library when his pocket jingle ran low before payday. So he was the one who soberly declared, "I read someplace about these Italian choirboys, no offense, who could sing higher than some gals as they grew up because . . . well, they didn't *have* no balls."

"*Castrati,*" Santini replied with a nod. "A dark chapter in the history of church music. By the way, I'm Polish on my mother's side. I can't see that wailing banshee as a true *castrato;* though. The Holy Father issued a papal bull against castrating choirboys about a hundred years ago. They were all volunteers even then. Some singers will sacrifice a lot for their art."

One of the mining men who'd held his ground asked, "What about some old boy who's lost his *nuts* but not his *muscles* in some awful accident? A disaster like that could make many a man go crazy and run through the empty galleries wailing like a banshee!"

A younger hand sporting high-heeled riding boots and a brace of Paterson Conversions declared, "What if it was a *critter*? I mind this tale by Mr. Edgar Allan Poe about this maniac who trains a big old ape to scamper up the sides of buildings in Paris, France."

"Wailing A over high C?" asked Santini dubiously.

To which the cowboy replied defensively, "Shoot, who's to say what a giant ape might wail like? There was nothing in that tale of the murders on Morgue Street about wailing. But Mr. Poe never said an ape *can't* wail, and what if that maniac in Paris, France, trained that particular ape to murder folks silent?"

Longarm tried to keep an open mind. But what Marshal Billy Vail called the process of eliminating made a trained ape sounding off in a high soprano tone unlikely.

Longarm held his torch up to note with satisfaction that whatever it was couldn't drop straight down at them because they were east of the worked-out lode, under solid rock.

He called a halt and asked Santini whether, speaking as a trained singer, he could say whether those banshee wails had come from another professional or not.

The tenor shrugged and said, "Tell me what you want me to say in court and I can swear to it either way with a clear conscience. If you want me to say he, she, or it was a real professional, the answer would be no. When I said A over high C, that was as close as one could describe the sound in musical terms. It was at least a quarter tone off, on the high side. On the other hand, if you want my opinion about voice lessons, nobody ever learned to hit that high a note just singing in the shithouse for the hell of it. I'd say you'd have to start with a strong natural voice in the soprano range, teach it to reach high enough to hurt, and then, as others have suggested, drive it mad. You couldn't pay any soprano I know to sustain such high notes for that long that often. It would wreck her throat and leave her laid up for days!"

Longarm said, "Sounded mighty loud to me too. But try her this way. What if that masked whatever had one of those

61

megaphone cones under that tattered shroud?"

Santini thought before he decided, "Might sound louder down here amid all these echoes. But shouting into a megaphone tends to *deepen* the town, not raise it *higher*. And how on earth would anybody scamper through those mine timbers like a monkey with a megaphone of any size in one hand?"

"Well, my boss calls such questions eliminating," Longarm said with a sigh.

Rothfeld said, "Somebody's headed this way from the lode!"

Longarm peered into the darkness of the Sutro to spy pinpoints of torchlight bounding closer and growing larger. He declared, "Everybody hold their fire. That's likely the searchers from on high."

He knew he was right when a distant voice called out, "Who's there and how come?"

Longarm called back, "U.S. Deputy Marshal Custis Long and a dozen others as foolhardy. If you gents are chasing that banshee we just ran up a hoist shaft, you missed her in the dark. She ain't come this way!"

The other party sloshed on toward them, grumbling and cussing until they could all make one another out in the flickering torchlight. Nat Rothfeld, being with the mining syndicate, knew the leaders of that other bunch and vice versa. It made things easier as Nat introduced the bunch of them. The leader who'd come down through the boxwork was a Cousin Jack or Cornishman named Crockett. One of the miners with him was Grogan, the survivor of that earlier banshee scare.

Nobody who knew the Consolidate Virginia works worth mentioning found it miraculous that the wailing whatever had slipped out from between the two search parties in the maze of treacherous unlit passageways.

Longarm said, "This Sutro tunnel is the only way out of the lower levels. How many exits might there be higher up on the mountain?"

Crockett said, "Fifteen or more if we're talking about the original old mine adits. Most have been boarded over or even filled with tailings since the different companies united, look you. An empty hoist shaft makes a lovely tip for waste rock, you see.''

Longarm nodded, but said, ''Such vague figures are made for a crook to work around, no offense. Are you saying nobody knows for certain how many ways there could still be in or out of the Comstock Lode?''

Crockett protested, ''Why would anyone keep records of adits nobody has worked for a generation, I pray thee?''

The Irishman who'd lost two pards to the banshee opined, ''How far would herself get in that gray costume within the glow of the A Street lamplight, bejasus? And if she *was* in the habit of leaving the tunnels above us, why would the boyos still be hearing her wails almost every other shift? She's still in the mine and growing bolder by the minute!''

As if to prove Grogan's point, they all heard a distant agonized scream followed by a muffled cackle of hyena laughter.

Grogan was not alone in making the sign of the cross.

Longarm said, ''Forget what I was just asking about other ways out. That's a moot question since the spooky thing seems intent on playing hide-and-seek in the dark.''

Crockett sighed and said, ''That tears it, look you! There's nowt to do now but climb all those ladders and start over again, please God!''

Grogan protested, ''Jesus, Mary, and Joseph, feel free to climb all them rungs you want, and I'm still off for some sleep after one hell of a day!''

Someone else asked if Consoidated Virginia was likely to pay them for all this overtime, and when Nat Rothfeld said he didn't know, Grogan was joined in his stand by more than half the men there.

Crockett protested, ''We can't let it get away, look you!''

To which another crusty hardrock man replied, ''Why not? Who can it hurt and what can it do with nobody working the night shift anymore?''

That was a good question, and Crockett was too smart a mining man to attempt an easy answer. He tried, ''That maniac is . . . *trespassing,* you see! It doesn't belong in the Consolidated Virginia or any silver mine at all, I'm sure.''

Longarm said, ''Back up and let's ride through that gate again. My boss, Marshal Vail, keeps telling us to consider a crook's *motive* as well as the means and opportunity. It won't matter how slick somebody moves about in the dark as soon as we figure out *how come!*''

Grogan said, ''Sure and that's easy. Whither the banshee is mortal or not, she's after scaring the bejasus out of us, and I'm off until I get some sleep and leave her to wail her darling heart out in an empty mine!''

As others made to follow the disgruntled Grogan, Longarm moved over to quietly warn Crockett, ''You'll lose them for good if you push it. They're too tired from getting nowheres to start all over right now!''

Crockett sighed and said, ''I know the feeling for I feel that way myself, look you! But I hate to just give up, and how would you go about it if you were in my place?''

Longarm said, ''Scientifically. Praise the Lord, this ain't my case. But if it was I'd commence with limelights, a heap of limelights at one end of the works, top to bottom, behind at least a squadron of fighting men, advancing in unison with all that light to show the way, until we swept the whole Comstock Lode from end to end, top to bottom.''

''And what if in the end there was nobody there?'' asked Crockett.

To which Longarm could only reply, ''I reckon I'd have to give serious thought to the notion of real haunts. I don't see how anyone mortal could keep from getting caught in such a sweep. On the other hand, I can't think of any other way to *catch* such a nimble whatever!''

Chapter 9

With only one twelve-hour shift still working the Comstock Lode, the steam-powered hoists weren't working, and nobody wanted to climb three thousand feet of ladders. So everybody came out of the Sutro and hiked back up to town the longer but less strenuous way. It took way longer to walk three miles uphill. So Longarm had lots of time to jaw with the others around him, and soon found himself trudging besides the star-drill hand called Grogan. When Grogan allowed he had indeed been the only survivor of that three-man tribute crew, Longarm got him to go over his story again. When they got to the part about Grogan and some others searching that remote gallery in vain for any traces of the banshee, Longarm said, ''It's been a spell since this child mucked ore, and I never worked tribute on my own. So we are talking about what you might call lawful *high-grading,* ain't we?''

Grogan replied in a defensive tone, ''Call it what you like and bad cess to yez all. Sure it's hard work, next to picking up a lump of pure metal and sticking it in yer pocket!''

Longarm said soothingly, ''I just now allowed tribute mining was lawful, and I never meant to imply it was easy. My point is that the banshee might have been out to scare the three of you away from a pocket of ore too modest in size for full-scale mining but rich enough to be worth what you three and who knows who else could gather like fallen fruit.''

Grogan snorted. ''Aroo, and did ye think nobody else was after thinking of that? When I gathered me wits and a dozen armed friends to go back up into that corner of the mine, the blossom rock we'd just blasted free when the banshee appeared was still there and all!''

''Every bit of it and all?'' asked Longarm dryly.

Grogan tripped over a sage clump in the moonlight, recovered, and trudged onward and upward, declaring, ''Jasus, Mary, and Joseph, and did ye think we took time to *assay* the blast-off with that murthering hell-fiend howling in our ears and all? It's possible somebody else lifted a pinch or more of native metal. But not enough to be worth the deaths of two foin men! The bunch of us salvaged two and a half tons of high-grade blossom rock in all, working shares. Once we got it up to Gould & Curry it assayed forty dollars a ton, which would have come to much more for the three of us than for a full dozen of us. The grains of gold were too fine to make out without a hand lens, and while there was far more silver, it had all gone black from the groundwater. So I'd be failing to see how any friends of the banshee could be hilping themselves to choice specimens of shattered rock in the dark and all.''

Longarm said, ''I can't see it either. Somebody told me another miner heard that banshee just before he was killed working alone.''

Grogan nodded grimly and said, ''Corrigan. A ton of rock moving the wrong way in the old Ophir galleries. I wasn't there, but the way they told me, Corrigan was another ambitious boyo inclined to tribute on his own time. He wasn't working by himself the evening he was after getting crushed. But he'd heard the banshee and told others before he was killed coming off shift a few evenings later.''

''You mean before he could go off on his own to work blossom rock?'' asked Longarm thoughtfully.

Grogan replied, ''Jasus! I hadn't thought of that! Are ye

saying herself, the banshee, doesn't *want* anybody working the blossom rock left behind in bonanza times?''

Longarm sighed and said, "I don't know that much about banshees, and this one ain't committed any federal offenses as far as I can see. So I reckon it's a matter for your company police and the state of Nevada. I only tagged along this evening because things were more tedious where I was just killing time. I'm supposed to be working another case for my Uncle Sam come midnight. At the rate we're going I ought to be back up to D Street by then.''

He was, with a few minutes to spare. He shook hands all around and parted friendly from the gents who'd climbed that long grade with him. When Enzio Santini invited Longarm to have a drink with him and Rothfeld, Longarm was tempted, but declined. He knew there was a taproom at the whorehouse he was headed for.

When he got to Madam Pearl's, that same pretty colored maid let him in and said she'd tell her boss lady he'd arrived if he'd make himself to home for a spell. So he ambled into the dimly lit red velvet taproom off the hallway.

As he did so, one of the shadowy male figures lounging about with a mess of half-dressed shady ladies jumped to his feet with both hands up and sobbed, "Don't throw down on me, Longarm! As God and all these other folks can see, I ain't spoiling for a fight and my Lightning is under the tail of my coat with nary a hand of mine anywheres *near* it!''

To which Longarm could only reply, "Aw, hang a wreath on your nose in memory of your dead brain, Jeff Otis. You ain't the one I'm here to see, and it wasn't me spreading all that bull about us having a showdown here in Virginia.''

The hired gun he'd brushed with aboard the stage from Reno pleaded, "Don't play cat and mouse with me if you don't mean that, Longarm! You know how other men who sit down to pee like to stir things up betwixt the likes of you and me. I swear to God I never told nobody I was out to clean your plow. I turned away from the Crystal Palace when another well-wisher told me you were yonder awaiting my pleasure. How was I to know you'd be coming *here* tonight? I swear nobody told me!"

Longarm said, "Watch your lingo in front of these ladies, and put your fool hands down before somebody mistakes this for a hold up. I know how the little kids egg on a schoolyard fight. Why don't we just belly up to yonder bar and make up? I don't know you well enough to kiss you."

Jeff Otis shook his head and allowed he'd forgotten he was supposed to meet somebody else at midnight. Longarm had no call to stop him as the hired gun slithered backwards from that taproom and tore out the front door.

Longarm shrugged and stepped over to the small corner bar to ask yet another half-dressed gal behind it whether she had any Maryland Rye.

She said, "I can serve you Magnolia Whiskey, and thanks for calling us ladies. I reckon you'd laugh if I told you I ain't always been what most gents call a soiled dove, huh?"

Longarm soberly replied, "Not hardly. I've yet to meet a lady in your line of work who started younger than eight or ten."

She sighed and poured him a shot as she confessed, "Thirteen. Neither of my older brothers trifled with flat-chested kids. It was my daddy who sold me to my first pimp. Daddy never screwed me. He was too religious to either trifle with such a warm-natured child or have her under the same roof with him. I reckon that why he's the only man in my family I still think about now and again."

Longarm sipped some whiskey, longing for a chaser but not anxious to give any other whorehouse tough an excuse to start up with him by calling him a sissy. As if she'd read his mind, the whore behind the bar asked if he'd care for some lager to go with that Magnolia.

He grudgingly allowed he might if it was on the house. She laughed and said Madam Pearl didn't charge for anything but the carnal pleasures upstairs. Longarm didn't ask how that policy tied in with a fugitive on the run from a federal warrant staying overnight and then some. He knew she'd tell him to ask her boss lady. He already had, and if they were lying they were lying.

That colored maid came in to tell Longarm Madam Pearl was ready to receive him now. So he followed her upstairs and into that plush back layout where, this time, the big blonde was reclining like Cleopatra on a red velvet chaise in a red sateen kimono. She wasn't wearing anything but red slippers under it. You could tell because she'd never bothered to fasten the sash when she'd put it on, and Longarm was reminded about that joke about a racy novel called *The Open Kimono* by Mr. Seymore Hare, although her bare thighs were sort of crossed and only one naked tit hung out completely.

As the maid left, closing the door behind her, Longarm removed his hat but remained standing as he calmly said, "Evening, Madam Pearl. I see you just got out of another tub. You said if I came back around this time, you'd be able to tell me when and where I can meet that gent High-grade Hal Diller tangled with downstairs."

She purred, "Why don't you sit down? Over here on this chaise with me, if you like."

Longarm stared over her tempting sprawl of half-naked blondness out into the darkness beyond the lace curtains in her bay window. He knew that with the lamps lit inside you'd be able to see in from outside. But on the other hand, the window faced east, and with each north-south street in Virginia City over thirty feet higher, east to west, there were probably no other windows facing hers, and nobody at a lower level would see anything but her pressed-tin ceiling.

Longarm saw that red tomato chair he'd perched on earlier seemed to be missing. He moved over and sat down closer to her slippers than her exposed pubic hair as he repeated his implied question about the local man who'd brushed with High-grade Hal and exposed his mighty cozy hideout—or to be fair, forced his casual-dressing landlady to call the law.

Madam Pearl asked, "What's the matter with us? Are you afraid of my size or disgusted by my past? Lord knows I'm

69

clean enough to eat off of, and more than one man has assured me I'm still pretty.''

Longarm placed his hat on the lamp table at his end of the chaise and assured her, ''You'll get no argument from this child on either of those points, ma'am. You're a right handsome woman, and I've never seen such a fiend for bath salts and toilet water.''

She sighed and said, ''They say pickpockets wash their hands more than any real dirt calls for too. I came West with a man who promised he'd make me an opera star. Looking back, I needed many a voice lesson to go with my natural talents as a sunny child who liked to sing. But you know how the rest of that story goes.''

Longarm raised a brow and declared, ''Not in detail, ma'am. You say you began in this business as an aspiring opera singer? Might you be able to hit the note of A over high C, if I'm recalling that correct?''

Madam Pearl sounded sincere enough as she laughed and told him he couldn't be recalling correctly. ''Hardly a soprano on Earth could range that high. *B* over high C would have gotten me into another career entirely. But, well, I was only another pretty girl with an untrained voice and a much more talented pussy. So it was only a few short steps from screwing our landlord when he came for the back rent to a trick now and then to pay for my so-called lover's booze and gambling, and then we wound up here in Virginia during bonanza times and I was saved from his weakness and my own stupidity by an older woman I shall always consider a saint. You've no doubt heard of the late Madam Julia Bulette, better known as the Darling of the Comstock?''

Longarm whistled and said, ''Everybody has. She was murdered back in '67 before I could ever meet up with her. I know some say the man they eventually hung for strangling her was a hero. But others say she was a good old gal, as well as mighty pretty.''

''Refined,'' said Madam Pearl with a sigh. ''As beautiful a profile as you'll ever see on any cameo brooch, but high-toned as a high-born lady in her ways—outside of bed, I mean. Sixteen carriages filled with the civic leaders and the whole fire department followed Madam Julia's hearse on the day of her funeral, and if the ladies of the DAR and WCTU didn't like it they could lump it. Madam Julia charged a thousand a night for her own pussy, and taught the few girls she was willing to offer guidance to to never forget a man wanted a tigress in bed but a lady of fine breeding to smoke and jaw with.''

Longarm nodded and said, ''I reckon she had us down about right. I can see how they made her an honorary fire chief. I've seen that one tintype of her posing with a fire helmet.''

Madam Pearl said, ''You'll note she wasn't *wearing* it. I was there when she posed for that portrait in a well-cut but conservative silk dress with the helmet on a table beside her. The boys from Hook and Ladder Number One wanted the picture to hang in their firehouse. She hailed from England and she'd lived in Louisiana before the war, and a failed marriage drove her into the horizontal trade she taught me so much about. So her speech was ever so refined, and her customers had to take a bath before she'd let any of us serve them.''

Longarm dubiously replied, ''I can see how some might figure a night with such a wonder was worth some money in bonanza times. How much might you have been charging High-grade Hal a night whilst he was here with you all?''

Madam Pearl made a wry face and said, ''I never said I was as good as Julia Bulette, and if I was, the bonanza days are long gone and, well, we do have overhead, even when nobody has much money to spend on pussy. So I was renting him a room with board and, all right, a little fun now and then for a hundred a week.''

Longarm said, ''That sounds like both of you should have been happy with the deal. Let's get back to that other customer who got into a fight with the outlaw and spoiled it for everybody. They were fighting over one of your gals called Joyce?''

Madam Pearl sat up straighter, spilling both big breasts out the front of her open kimono as she said, ''They told me you had a memory for names and faces. You did that without looking at your notebook. A girl with a shady past has to watch her step around a man like you, Custis Long.''

Longarm shrugged and said, ''Peddling pussy ain't a federal crime, no offense. But holding back evidence could be so considered, if you get my meaning.''

She swung her slippers off the chaise to sit closer to him as she replied in a husky tone, ''I could level with you if I knew for certain nothing I said could be used to put me in prison, handsome.''

He told her to spell it out if she expected him to say yes or no to some sort of deal in exchange for her evidence.

She smiled dirty and said flat out, ''I want you to fuck me before I talk. One of the first things Madam Julia taught us was that no lawman can lay a finger on you in court after he's had his dick in you in your own bed. I want to be sure you won't arrest me along with anybody else I may be able to put you in touch with. So how about it? Do you want to fuck me or just go fuck yourself for all I care?''

Longarm slowly rose to his full considerable height as he peeled off his frock coat and unbuckled his gunbelt, muttering, ''I swear to God, there seems no end to the sacrifices I'm expected to make in the name of the law.''

To which Madam Pearl coyly replied, leaning back against the head of the red velvet chaise with her big bare thighs spread wide in welcome, ''I know sometimes it's hard. But somebody's got to do it. So show it hard and let's *do* it, lawman!''

Chapter 10

He'd gotten it halfway up by the time he'd gotten all the way out of his duds because Madam Pearl had risen to her own considerable height to shuck her kimono and move over like a Greek statue come to life and take the matter in hand, kissing him on the lips like an old chum as they both sat down on the red velvet. That sure felt swell on a man's bare ass and balls.

As the big blonde rolled half atop him to part his thighs with her knees and sink slowly between them while she kissed her way down his chest and belly, Longarm assured her he was hard enough to get it in without any French lessons.

She murmured, "Don't rush things, my impetuous youth. Let Teacher lead the way. I can see it's hard. I can see how much of it you brought to school for Teacher too, and I just had a vinegar douche getting undressed for company. So whether you think we need any lubrication or not, we're still going to start out nice and wet, dear."

Then she couldn't say anything else because her mouth was full, and Longarm's earlier observations about professionals doing things so fine for pleasure certainly applied in her case to the crime against nature defined on most states' statute books as *fellatio*, which was Latin for "I suck."

Madam Pearl committed fellatio better than most gals knew how, not having any way to know what it really felt like.

Somebody—he hoped it been the late Julia Bulette—had instructed the big blonde to purse her lush lips over her teeth and pucker them into an imitation asshole she kept wet with her darting tongue as she slid the tight ring of soft wetness up and down his shaft while she tickled the bottom with that same squirmy tongue. He could tell she'd practiced the art to the point where, like a sword swallower but unlike most willing women, she could take the excited head past the gagging point between her tonsils and on down her throat, where the swallowing contractions seemed to be driving them both crazy.

He came that way, as most mortal men might have, dead or alive, and then she kissed her way back up him, growling that he had *her* gushing, and proving it by spitting her wet crotch on his trembling shaft and biting down on it with her warm innards just as their lips met again. He started to gag when she shoved her tongue back in his mouth, but then he could tell she'd swallowed more than once on her way up his gut, and who really cared when they were being sucked that hard by a big bouncing blonde's old ring-dang-do?

She must have had good ears. Longarm hadn't been humming the old trail song out loud in time with her bumps and grinds, but she must have heard, or else great minds really flowed in the same channels. For the next thing Longarm knew she'd shoved a nipple in his mouth, leaned back with her bare arms around him, and proceeded to bay like a coyote at the pressed-tin ceiling:

"You naughty girl, her mother said,
You've gone and lost your maidenhead,
There's only one thing left to do,
Go advertise your ring-dang-do!

So she went to the city, to be a whore,
She hung a sign above her door,
One dollar down and the rest when through,
That's how she sold her ring-dang-do!"

74

Then she commenced to bawl like a baby as she buried her blond head in the crook of his neck and naked shoulder while she just crouched across his lap with a big thigh out to either side and his now-raging erection up inside her immobile innards.

So they wound up on the shag rug with him on top to finish right as he kissed her tear-soaked eyelids, assuring her everything would be all right in a gentle tone while he banged her as any natural man would have and, he suspected, as she wanted him to.

He knew he'd guessed right when she suddenly smiled in wonder through her tears and murmured, "Oh, shit, I think I'm going to come!"

"Wasn't that the general intent?" he asked conversationally without missing a beat.

She sounded almost as casual as she began to bump and grind again with her vaginal muscles gripping tight and then letting go for a better grip as he thrust in and out. She said, "As a matter of fact, I wanted to make sure you'd be compromised as the arresting officer. I've laid many another john good for less serious reasons. Madam Julia taught us that as long as you were being ridden in any case, it was only good sense to give a good short ride instead of a long drawn-out ordeal for the both of you."

Longarm gasped, "I'm glad Madam Julia died before my time. Doing a thing this fine with the teacher as taught *you* could be injurious to a man's health and . . . Powder River and let her buck if I ain't almost there!"

She moaned that that made the two of them, and seemed as surprised as she was pleasured by such a shock to her system. As Longarm kept it moving in her after they'd both come, the big blonde shuddered under him and croaked, "Thank God I don't have to screw the customers myself these days. You could ruin a working girl for the night with that big sweet tool of yours, and I can see why they call you Long *Arm*. A completely accurate description would never be fit for the *Union*

75

or *Enterprise* to set in type. Could we go into the other room and get in bed now? I want some more, but you're not exactly a lapdog and this fucking floor is too hard for serious fucking!''

Longarm laughed, allowed he hadn't noticed that they were only feeling one another up, and got off to haul her erect before he swept her off her feet to tote into her inner sanctum. She laughed girlishly, and allowed she was glad he still had that much strength left.

But as they began once more atop the covers of her four-poster by dimmer light dog-style, Longarm was starting to feel as disgusted with himself as he knew Marshal Vail's old woman and President Hayes's First Lady might, as his first glow of lust was cooled some by the common sense that only came over a man after a warm meal and a fine lay in the same evening. So gripping an ample hip in either hand as he drove his battering ram just fast enough to keep it hard, Longarm brought up the subject of that witness she said she'd put him together with. He said, "I doubt any court in the land would allow this child to appear against such a delicate flower after abusing her fair white body this vilely, Madam Pearl."

She arched her spine and bit down with her love muscles to reply in a teasing tone, "He made me do it, Your Honor! If it please the court, he made me blow him and fucked me thrice before I gave in to his thirst for knowledge!"

Longarm snorted, "Aw, come on, Pearl! Nobody can say I ain't been a good sport up to now. But you're commencing to piss me off!"

She said, "Finish right and kiss me like you really like me, and I'll send for the man you want to talk to."

He withdrew and rolled her on her back as he demanded, "He's here right now?"

She pulled him down into her and wrapped her long legs around her waist as she confessed, "He's been here all along. I told him earlier you'd be here around midnight. He said that gave him plenty of time with Joyce and that he'd be down in the taproom awaiting your pleasure because he has nothing to hide from anybody but his wife.''

''You sassy minx!'' Longarm laughed. ''What was all this bull about my compromising myself with you like this if that other man was willing to talk all this time? The two of you ain't involved in anything Uncle Sam might be worried about, are you?''

Madam Pearl gripped him tighter and assured him, ''Shit, I haven't even done *this* with him. I told you my part in a brawl between customers downstairs. He says he has nothing to hide either. But one of my girls used to work for Madam Ruth Jacobs in Denver, and she told me you never paid for pussy and were reputed to be hung like a horse by the working girls of Colorado. So have I asked you for a dime, and won't you shove that one-eyed trouser-snake up my ring-dang-do just one more time before I die?''

He said he would, and he did. Madam Julia's point about just getting it over with was well taken, although by the time she'd come again he was just starting to get there again, and didn't feel another serious try would be worth the effort—or the danger that he'd have her hot again by the time he could make it.

So he pretended to join her as she came the last time, or said she had, seeing she seemed to be setting herself up for a brag.

Back in Denver both Madam Ruth Jacobs and her arch-rival, Madam Emma Gould, told everybody they'd been had all three ways by the one and original Longarm. But he knew none of his real friends believed them.

She finally had enough mercy on him to let him get dressed and sit out on that chaise with a fresh cheroot while she went out to fetch that witness with her kimono fastened more chastely now.

Longarm rose and threw open one sash of her bay window to the night air in hopes of airing away the pungent aftermaths of perfumed sweat and fornication.

He saw he'd guessed right about the housing across the way.

To peek at Madam Pearl spread out on that chaise, a body would have to stand on a box atop the flat top of the mansard roof of another place facing the next street down the slope. He was just as glad nobody had watched him being so weak-willed earlier.

Madam Pearl came back in with an older gent combining the costume and airs of a sourdough made up by Mark Twain with a small-town bigwig running for alderman. Madam Pearl introduced him as Boomer Barnes, the discoverer of the famous Little Pittsburgh near Leadville.

When they shook, the self-confident Boomer Barnes had a firm shake to go with his sincere smile. So Longarm said, "We ain't going to get along if you draw the longbow on me, Boomer. As a Colorado rider who gets sent up to Leadville on business now and again, I have it on good authority that the Little Pittsburgh vein was struck by a Dutchman by the name of Rische."

Barnes nodded easily and said, "Then you must know he had some help. August Rische come up to Leadville as a total greenhorn who couldn't speak English worth mention and knew more about cobbling shoes than prospecting for color. He was pulling on a jug under a pine tree with another greenhorn named George Hook. They'd been grubstaked by old Hod Tabor, who extended credit to gobs of prospectors trading at his general store in Leadville. I know the tale they tell about the way Silver Dollar Tabor wound up with the whole blamed Little Pittsburgh. Some of it's true. A fool and his money are soon parted, and Tabor bought Hook and Rische out with extra cash he raised from the sale of paper shares in the silver still in the ground. You'll have heard how big mining moguls such as Moffat and Chaffee horned in to do wonders and eat cucumbers. But do they sing the praises of the prospector who told those two greenhorns there was color under that one pine tree and not a surface outcrop anywheres else on that hilltop? They do not, because I am not one to brag. But ask either Hook or Rische who stopped by for a pull on that jug with them that afternoon, watched where he was spitting, and told them where to dig!''

Longarm said, ''I mean to. Tell us how you happened to know High-grade Hal Diller well enough to tangle with him down in the taproom.''

Boomer Barnes looked surprised as he replied, ''I just told you I've prospected all about Leadville and the headwaters of the Arkansas. I never drank with High-grade Hal. He sure never worked for me. I'd heard he was a crook before he got arrested a spell back. I'd heard he'd been sent to Jefferson Barracks. So you can imagine my surprise when we met downstairs the other night.''

''They got into it over Joyce,'' explained Madam Pearl.

Boomer Barnes shook his head and said, ''You just heard the lawman say he wants nothing but the truth, Madam Pearl.''

Turning back to Longarm, the prospector said, ''Joyce would never go upstairs with another john if I was on the premises. It ain't just that I'm so good-looking. I never wear my boots in bed or try to get out of paying for extra pleasures. I told some of the others we'd been fighting over a gal after Madam Pearl here threw him out for drawing on me. I don't mind saying that startled me. I thought I'd told him friendly why we didn't need and couldn't afford to hire him.''

''To do what?'' Longarm asked.

Boomer Barnes said, ''Blast and muck. Me and two side-kicks have been following a lead I struck a mile around the mountain from where the Comstock Lode pinches out, or appears to. We might be fooling ourselves with no more than a crack in the formation, filled with blossom bleeding off the main lode. We're hoping to find another lode entire, and won't our grandchildren have something to brag on if we do! Meanwhile, like I said, we're barely mining enough bullion betwixt the three of us to pay our expenses if we just invest our sweat. The last thing we need is a workforce aiming to draw day wages, and if we *did* want to hire an extra hand, he'd be a good, hard worker, not a convicted high-grader out to help himself to our hard-earned color!''

Longarm nodded thoughtfully and said, "High-grade Hal's wanted for more than pocketing rich ore samples. So I can see why nobody digging a mine large or small would want him anywhere near it. He must be low on pocket jingle by now. A man has to need a job desperately before he's inclined to take a turndown so personally."

Turning to Madam Pearl, Longarm asked her if she or any of her gals had heard anything about High-grade Hal turning up anywhere else to apply for pussy or a job.

She said she'd have no call to cover for the bad-tempered cuss. So Longarm turned back to Boomer Barnes to say, "I was just this evening chasing a haunt who seems interested in high-grade blossom rock too."

The prospector nodded and said, "We heard about that banshee over in the Comstock galleries. Can't say we've had her howling in *our* ears so far. Our shaft can't be more than twenty feet into the mountain. You can still see daylight from the working face. I don't think that spook is after any sort of ore. I think somebody is playing on the old country notions of some mining men to keep them out of certain parts of the old galleries."

Longarm asked, "To what end? What could that banshee or the mastermind putting somebody up to acting like one be hiding somewhere in the depths of this mountain?"

Boomer Barnes laughed and said, "I don't even know what's ten feet deeper than we've sunk our shaft so far. We're talking miles and miles of deserted drifts nobody's been through officially in years. You name it and I reckon I could hide it, guarded by a banshee, somewhere in all that deep dark confusion. But nobody's asked me to hide toad squat in any hole in the ground, and all I've got to show you, if you'd care to look, is a modest shaft with a little color and hardly a banshee worth mention up to now."

Chapter 11

It was after one in the morning. Red Robin had likely gone back to her hotel and fallen asleep by then, and it wasn't as if he was suffering a raging erection. But Longarm had told Red Robin he'd join her later if he could, and nobody was holding a gun to his head as he left Madam Pearl's. So dropping by and hoping Red Robin had dropped off might be easier in the end than lying to a pal.

So despite a certain stiffness to his walk and no stiffness at all between his legs, Longarm strode on past his hotel to where Red Robin was staying closer to the opera house.

Her hotel was bigger, with more than one entrance, the way traveling salesmen and theatrical folks who kept odd hours liked things. Having no call to sully a single guest's reputation, Longarm never went near the room desk. He just strode across the dimly lit lobby as if he owned the blamed hotel, and almost made it to the stairwell before a familiar voice from behind him asked whether he was staying there or looking for a part in *Norma,* if the scenery ever got to town.

Longarm turned to face the small brunette Lili FitzRoy and her pal, the auburn-haired Flora Livingston. He could smell the liquor on their breaths at conversing distance. That likely accounted for them being up and abroad and unescorted at such an hour. Longarm ticked his hat brim to them but didn't say what he was doing there. The best way to argue with drunks, or women in any state of consciousness, was to say as little as possible and let them fill in the blanks as they saw fit. They were going to in any case, and they were less likely to yell if they had the floor undisputed.

Lili said, "We left the party at the Crystal Palace. Some of the others were still waiting for you and Enzio to come back and tell us what all that fuss about something down in the mine was about. But we weren't having any fun. So we came on home, and what do you want to do now?"

Longarm said, "I'm on duty, hunting for fugitives from justice at the moment. You say Mr. Santini never came back to the Palace? We parted friendly hours ago here in town."

"Maybe he's with Miranda," Flora Livingston suggested, raising one hand to politely hide a yawn.

The just as drunk but more wide awake Lili replied, "A lot of good that does lonely little you and me! You should have let me invite that nice cowboy we were talking to to walk us home, you spoilsport!"

Flora Livingston said, "I was holding out for a sailor, and now I'm off to bed before I fall down right here!"

Lili murmured to Longarm, "Help me get her up those stairs. I think she means it, and we can't leave her down here to sleep it off!"

Longarm started to make some excuse. Then he saw that the auburn-haired Flora had shut both eyes and seemed to be going over like a ponderosa sawed off at the bottom. So he moved in to grab her as she purred, "Do you really like Wagner's *Sturm und Drang* that much?" Then she started to seriously sag, and he swept her up in his arms and asked Lili to lead the way.

The brunette sighed, "It's not fair. I saw him first!" Then she went up the stairs ahead of Longarm and his shapely limp burden. Halfway up, the one he was carrying softly sighed, "You will be gentle and you promise to respect me in the morning, right?"

Longarm didn't answer. Although her question raised more

interest in such matters than he'd thought he still possessed at that hour.

He followed Lili along the second-story hall. He was wondering how he'd help her with that key unless he put her pal down. Then she got it in the lock, turned it, and left it in the door as she tottered on to the bedstead to flop facedown across it.

She was snoring as Longarm gently laid Flora down beside her. The one who'd appeared more ready to pass out still had enough life in her to dreamily ask him if he'd get her going with some lap-licking before he went all the way. Longarm knew that on some lonesome night on the range in a bedroll he was going to curse himself severely, but at the moment it seemed best to take that key out of the lock, place it inside the room away from the door, and lock the two of them safely inside with a blade of his pocketknife that could get anyone but a lawman arrested.

Then he moved back to the stairs and mounted them to the top floor, where Red Robin was as likely to be awake and pissed as sleeping off a long evening at the Crystal Palace. He had a time reading the room numbers by the dim light of one oil lamp down the hall. When he got to Red Robin's number, there was no light shining under the door from the far side. So he heaved a sigh of relief and started to turn away.

Then he had a better notion. He commenced to pick her lock with yet another clever blade as he considered how he'd be killing more than a single bird with the same stone if he could manage it so Red Robin could wake up with him next to her in bed, after a good night's sleep, thanks to his considerate nature.

He cracked the door softly open and eased inside in the dark on the balls of his feet, recalling that time on Sherman Street when a Denver widow woman had praised him as an understanding lamb, just after he'd told her he'd be content to just hold her through the night, seeing it was that time of the month for her and he'd just had an unexpected run-in with that new stenographer at the Federal Building.

But when he eased over to the bedstead he found it empty. Red Robin wasn't home yet and it was well past her quitting time. Longarm moved to the window overlooking the front entrance. The street lamps had mostly burned out for the night. But the moon was shining bright, while hither and yon late-burning lamps tossed squares of brighter light across the deserted dirt street and plank walks.

He figured Red Robin had likely loitered for a late supper or even a few rounds of drinks at the bar with the boys. Red Robin was paid to get on with her audience, although she made it a point not to let her audience get aboard her. So Longarm explored her hired corner room as he waited up for her. He wasn't surprised to find a small but up-to-date modern bathroom keeping company with a walk-in closet. Red Robin was almost as devoted to tub baths as Madam Pearl, and had a lot of wardrobe for a gal who never appeared in anything but a red velvet ball gown. He found a big steamer trunk in that closet. It was locked. He didn't care. He'd seen most every stitch Red Robin ever wore, and vice versa. He went back in the bathroom and took a leak in the fancy commode, staring out the open window in the dark as he did so. Longarm could remember when even rich folks had to piss in chamber pots and crap out back in the yard. Working-class and poor folks still did. It felt sinfully luxurious to be able to piss indoors, pull the chain, and just forget all about it.

He'd shaken the dew off his rosebud and pulled that chain when, out on C Street, he spied the familiar outline of Red Robin, her velvet gown looking black by moonlight, as she and some galoot came along the far side arm in arm.

Longarm told himself she'd naturally asked somebody where she worked to escort her home in the dark. Sure she had. That was how come they were walking so tight, as if joined at the hip.

"Perfidity, thy name is woman!" Longarm sighed as he turned from the commode to button his damned pants and get out of there. It was a free country, and Longarm wasn't up to either a duel for the favors of a wandering piano player, or those drawing-room comedy conversations where a dude let on he didn't mind another gent playing musical beds with him. Red Robin had gone off with others in the past, and the Good Lord knows she could accuse him of the same. So he slipped out of her quarters and headed for the stairs. Then it came to him he'd likely meet Red Robin and her gentleman of the moment on those stairs if he chanced that way out.

He crawfished back the other way, hoping for a nook or cranny he could flatten out in. He'd just given up when he noticed there was no number on the door directly across from Red Robin's. He tried the knob. It turned and opened to reveal the innards of a broom closet. Longarm had to bend at the knees to get his head in under a cross-shelf loaded with buckets and such. But he'd managed, with the door a crack ajar, as he heard Red Robin's familiar voice on the stairs.

As she and her unexpected escort came down the hall toward him, Red Robin was insisting, "You're wasting your time. I told you I barely know Custis Long, and even if I knew him a whole lot more, he'd never come calling after one in the morning! Why don't we forget all this before you wind up in a whole lot of trouble? Deputy Long's not the only man in town who's likely to take my side if you do anything mean to me, good sir!"

Longarm recognized the other voice as it growled, "I told you I had no intent on harming one hair on your dear little pussy, as long as we do things my way and my way alone."

It was good to hear Jeff Otis didn't know Red Robin shaved down yonder. But he was still a son of a bitch, and Longarm had just about run out of patience.

So he waited for Red Robin to unlock her door and step inside first, as the lady was supposed to. Then the professional gunslick messed up Longarm's first plan. So he had to come up with another, fast, when Otis suddenly shoved Red Robin to one side but hung on to her, the son of a bitch, entering her room ahead of her behind the muzzle of his own drawn .38 Colt Lightning.

Longarm slid silently from his hidey-hole, .44-40 in hand,

just as Red Robin's door slammed shut in his face. He stood there muttering a lot of mean things about Jeff Otis, back to all his great-grandmothers, then waited until he saw lamplight under the door and heard Red Robin trill, "You see? I told you he wouldn't be here! Make yourself at home. I'll be right back."

"Where do you think you're going?" asked the surly Otis, who was closer to the door.

Red Robin sweetly replied, "To take a piss in yonder pissery! I'd let you watch but I don't know you that well. Are you afraid I'll go out a fourth-floor window and fly away like a bat?"

Jeff Otis laughed cruelly and said, "I wouldn't put it past you. You've already lied to me about your lover boy. Leave the door open if you really have to piss."

Red Robin protested, "Aw, come on, be a gent and let a lady have a little privacy! I couldn't do that in front of a strange man, or a man I knew better, if the truth be told!"

Jeff Otis replied in a tone of pretended indifference, "Just hold it till I finish with Longarm, then. You can piss all over his body for all I care once I'm gone."

Longarm wondered if Red Robin could see that nobody aimed to ambush a man in a lady's chambers and leave that same lady alive to bear witness. If she did, she never let on as she protested, "No shit, I really have to take a piss!"

Otis told her to go ahead. Longarm could hear Red Robin's angry footsteps as she marched to the adjoining bath and threw the door open. Then Longarm heard the door he couldn't see slamming shut as Jeff Otis yelled, "Open that damn door or so help me, I'll empty my wheel through it, hear?"

To which a distant muffled voice replied, "Fuck you!" in a superior ladylike tone.

So Jeff Otis was pumping bullets through the bathroom door when Longarm kicked in the hall door to pump three rounds in Jeff Otis as the wild-eyed gunslick whirled to train his own smoking six-gun Longarm's way. Then, as Otis fell back against a dresser, weakly trying to raise his own muzzle as he fought to stay on his feet, the bathroom door popped open and Red Robin came out like a cuckoo-clock bird to blast a pearl-handled and nickel-plated derringer right in the dying man's ear.

That finished him off for sure, and made an awful mess on the rug as Otis flopped down atop his scattered brains and bits of hairy skull fragments.

"That'll learn him!" Red Robin chortled, smoking derringer in hand. Longarm commenced to reload his bigger weapon as he quietly told her, "I was hoping to take him alive. Or alive enough to clear up a few matters for us leastways."

Somewhere in the night an alarm triangle was clanging. They didn't have as much gunplay in Virginia as some cow towns were used to. Red Robin said, "There's no mystery here. His name was Jeff Otis and he started telling folks the two of you were at feud the moment he got to town. He was waiting outside when I quit at the saloon a few minutes ago. He threw down on me and walked me home at gunpoint. The rest you seem to know. Where were you whilst I was diving into my bathtub to get at my garter holster just now?"

Longarm said, "Broom closet, then the hall, until it was safe to assume you'd be out of the lines of fire. He'd set us up for a sort of love-triangle killing if they caught him before he could get out of town. He started up with me on sight this morning. Made war talk all over town, and just this evening accused me of spoiling for trouble with such a peaceful soul. So the general plan called for you and me down there on the carpet instead of him. He meant to evoke the unwritten law allowing a man to defend his fool self when a fight over a gal turned ugly. He might have told any number around the Crystal Palace how sincere his admiration for you was next to my roughshod bullying. I'm glad we're both fully dressed right now. This place is fixing to be crawling with the local law and reporters from both papers any minute now."

As if to prove his point, they could hear police whistles and shouts out front. Someone in the hall was calling, "Down at the far end! You can smell the gunsmoke from here!"

Red Robin finished reloading her own ladylike weapon, and hoisted her red velvet skirts to put it back in its holster on the inside of one lush thigh as Longarm put his own gun away and told her, "Let me do all the talking. I've been through this routine a time or more, and it can save a lot of paperwork when you word things true but simple."

She said, "Go ahead. I don't see anything complicated about a known gun for hire laying for a well-known lawman in the quarters of an old pal."

Longarm sighed and said, "That's because you ain't a lawman, old pal. You described him right just now as a hired gun. So the real question before the house is who in blue blazes *hired* him. I somehow fail to see him going to all that fancy footwork just for *practice*!"

Chapter 12

As the place filled up with lawmen and the just plain nosy, it got tough to determine who rode for the town law or Consolidated Virginia's company police. Longarm wasn't sure there was much difference.

He told anyone who asked the same story as Red Robin held her tongue. He didn't lie to fellow lawmen. But to spare Red Robin's rep, he felt no call to volunteer details nobody asked. So he got full credit for all the damage done to the late Jeff Otis, and nobody could deny, after one look at the dents in Red Robin's bathtub and the way they lined up with those bullet holes in the door, that Longarm had doubtless saved the piano player's life from a spurned admirer gone loco.

More than one witness from the Crystal Palace came forward to say they'd noticed Jeff Otis forcing his attentions on the popular piano player when he'd come tearing in out of the dark after midnight. When nobody asked Longarm how come he'd followed the two of them back to her hotel, he never said he had or hadn't.

It was going on three in the morning by the time things started to calm down again. They'd hauled the body out, and the hotel's night man had roused some Mexicans to change the carpet and mop the floor in Red Robin's room. But there were still some company dicks and town deputies loitering about, along with other guests aroused by the gunplay. So when Red Robin took Longarm aside and said they'd best say good night discreetly, he nodded soberly and allowed he'd get on back to his own hotel. Somebody had already said something about a coroner's inquest after a good night's sleep.

Red Robin sighed and smiled wistfully up at him, declaring, "You're so understanding for such a horny natural man, Custis. I want you so bad right now that it's running down my thigh. But it would be all over town before you took it out, and think how horny we'll both feel by the time we're free to do it. What was that bullshit about a coroner's inquest just now?"

He made sure nobody was close enough to overhear as he quietly told her, "Bullshit. But in spite of Ned Buntline's *Wild West Magazine*, you ain't supposed to just order a round of drinks after you gun a man, either in self-defense or just for the heck of it. The county coroner has to put down the probable cause on the death certificate before the probate judge gets to settle the estate of the corpse. That's what they call it when they use any cash a dead stranger has on him to pay for his burial and any other cleanup—probating his estate."

He caught the concerned look in her eye and added, "Don't fret your pretty little self about it, kitten. I don't want you to have to lie under oath either. Just tell the truth about Otis throwing down on you outside the Crystal Palace and insisting on walking you home. You really didn't know where I was at the time. So you won't have to say. Just tell them that as soon as you got upstairs you ducked into your bath, slammed the door in his face, and jumped in the tub as he fired at you through the door."

Red Robin brightened and said, "Right! The next thing I knew there came the dulcet roar of your bigger gun, and I came out to discover I'd been saved from a fate worse than death!"

Longarm smiled thinly and replied, "I ain't sure there's any fate worse than death. But that does sound poetic if you want to toss it in."

So they shook on it, in deference to her rep, and Longarm went back to his own hotel near Taylor Street for the novelty of some time in bed alone.

He got close to six hours sleep in two sections. When the Consolidated Virginia steam whistle woke him up at dawn, along with everybody else on the mountain, he rose long enough to take a piss, and then he ignored his morning hard-on to flop back down and sleep some more, until he was awakened at nine by a bullwhip fight out front between two ore-wagon teamsters.

The one hauling a load toward the stamping mills prevailed over the other driving the empty back to the adit after some of the crowd that had gathered to watch started yelling that he was a thoughtless asshole to argue with a man who had tradition on his side.

Longarm washed up, shaved his own chin at the sink, and got dressed. He'd already cleaned his .44-40 before calling it a night in the wee small hours. But he stripped it and went over it with a clean patch by the better light of day before he reloaded and strapped it back on. He hadn't fired the double derringer clipped to one end of his gold-washed watch chain. But he looked it over and gave it a wipe as long as he had the time. You hardly ever got the time to make sure your guns would fire when it came to actually fire them, and they'd allowed that that coroner's hearing would be called after the noon dinner hour, with the exact time to be posted over on the town bulletin board in front of City Hall.

So Longarm had plenty of time to send a mess of wires after a light breakfast of fried eggs over chili con carne with a side order of buckwheat pancakes under sorghum syrup.

He moseyed over to City Hall to see that, sure enough, they'd called that coroner's inquest for three P.M. He saw his own name on the list of witnesses to be called, along with Red Robin, the night clerk from her hotel, and three gents who'd seen her leave work the night before with the late Jeff Otis. They naturally listed the coroner's jury as well. So when Longarm went over to the Crystal Palace to reassure Red

Robin, he knew what he was talking about when he bellied up to the bar beside Nat Rothfeld to say, "Howdy. I see you're sitting in judgment on me this afternoon, Nat."

The accountant had his snooty college accent back as he signaled the barkeep for a round and said, "Mere formality. Some company guns I can vouch for told me this morning what happened last night. I was on the Reno stage when that idiot started up with you. Would it help if I recused myself as a juror to bear witness for you?"

Longarm said, "I wish you wouldn't. I'd rather have a pal judging my story than backing it. Otis was wandering all over town making war talk about me. I'd as soon leave it at that than drag in any ladies."

Rothfeld nodded and said, "I see no reason why that little brunette opera singer should be forced to testify either. So tell me, what's the story about you and Red Robin?"

Longarm reached for the shot glass beside his beer schooner with a nod of thanks and asked innocently, "What's the story you've heard?"

The accountant laughed lightly and said, "Opinion seems divided. She has a rep for spurning the advances of the men where she works. On the other hand, some say you had it on with the Divine Sarah when she and her French theatrical out-fit toured Nevada."

Longarm swallowed the Jack Daniels, chased it with local lager, and soberly said, "You have my word as a man I never got frisky with Miss Sarah Bernhardt, a national treasure of France. The State Department had us keep an eye on her when they heard some ugly talk about the good old gal's religious persuasion."

Rothfeld nodded and said, "I'm glad you told me that. They tell me you saved Sarah Bernhardt from Jew-baiters out to assassinate her not too far from here."

Longarm shrugged modestly and said, "In point of fact, the gent who ought to get most of the credit was a serious outlaw who'd changed his name and his own Hebrew birth for public consumption. I can't tell you who he was. He swore me and

Miss Sarah to secrecy as he lay dying in her arms. Suffice it to say, the fanatic who couldn't abide the national treasure of France touring this land of the free didn't know the gun for hire was as Jewish or more. Miss Sarah doesn't deny being born, out of wedlock to a Dutch lady of the Hebrew persuasion in Paris, France. Miss Sarah told me she suspected her daddy might have been a law student whose name escapes me. She said her momma named her Rosine before she palmed her off on others to raise. Somewhere along the line she wound up in a Papist convent school, and took to the faith of some kindly nuns without having to give the matter much thought. She's never denied her mother was a not-too-religious whore of the Hebrew persuasion, or that they'd changed the spelling of the Dutch Van Hard to the more French-sounding Bernhardt. But she said she didn't understand why some kept saying she was a Jewish whore, seeing nobody had ever called her mother a Catholic actress."

Rothfeld laughed and said he didn't either. Then he said, "We've followed some of your suggestions about limelights over in the mine. So tell me what you found out down at Madam Pearl's last night."

Longarm signaled for the round he was buying as he smiled thinly and said, "Word sure gets around when you ride for the outfit that runs the town. I met up with that customer who knew High-grade Hal of old. He tells it a tad different than Madam Pearl and her girls. But things add up about the same."

"Do you think Boomer Barnes would tell the truth if it was in his own favor not to?" asked the Consolidated Virginia man.

Longarm raised a brow as well as his fresh-filled shot glass as he replied, "You do have your own spies out, don't you? I've already wired some pals in Leadville about Boomer. But I'll be surprised if they wire back they never heard of him, and I know for a fact High-grade Hal Diller has a bad rep among Leadville mining men. So what call would even a bullshit artist from Leadville have for saying he'd refused a job to a known ore thief?''

The mining company accountant shrugged, washed down his own whiskey, and said, ''I wouldn't trust either one of those reputed mining men as far as I could spit against the wind. I've never met High-grade Hal. But who am I to argue with those who have that he's not a crook?''

He sipped more suds and added, ''As for Boomer Barnes, we just don't know what he and his shifty-eyed sidekicks might be up to, but it has to be something larcenous. They've staked a claim where others have been over the same ground and found nothing worth claiming. Can you imagine a square yard of Mount Davidson that wasn't combed for assay samples during the frantic rush of the early sixties? Everyone from Paiute Indians to newspaper reporters called Mark Twain panned for color all the way up to the Truckee in those days, pissing in the pans when there was no other running water. So how in hell could anyone have missed an outcrop of blossom rock just a mile or so beyond that one end of the thoroughly explored Comstock Lode?''

''North end or south end?'' asked Longarm. ''Boomer never said last night.''

Rothfeld replied without hesitation, ''North end—out past Chinatown Canyon, as a matter of fact. What difference might that make?''

''Sunlight,'' Longarm replied. ''The big California rush got started when a ditch digger named Marshal noticed sunlight glinting off gold mixed with wet gravel in the raceway of Sutter's mill. Might have took him longer to spy color if they'd been working on a cloudy day or on the north slope of a mountain. But have it your way and let's say Boomer and his pals are wrong, or lying, about a new strike close enough to matter. My boss, Marshal Billy Vail, preaches we should look for motives, means, and opportunity. I'd say Boomer Barnes had both the time and skills required to dig a hole in the ground and call it a mine. After that, we're left with why he'd want to *do* such a thing. Has he been offering any mining shares for sale without any assay reports to back 'em up?''

Rothfeld scowled down at his empty shot glass and held up two fingers as he grumbled, "No. To give the devil his due, my syndicate offered to buy out the claim and they turned us down. I take it this conversation is, ah . . . private?''

Longarm shook his head and said, "Not hardly, if you're talking about any federal offenses. I'm a federal lawman, and I reckon I'd better pass on a third shot of whiskey for now. You were saying Boomer Barnes is a crook because he turned down a deal you'd as soon I kept confidential?''

The accountant protested, "Don't go putting words in my mouth if you don't want me asking awkward questions at that coroner's inquest this afternoon! Whatever gave you the idea Consolidated Virginia had a thing to hide about that old sourdough's so-called mining claim?''

Longarm sipped more beer and said, "You did. Nobody ever tells a pal to keep it confidential that he ain't been screwing said pal's old woman. So let me guess, and feel free to ask anything you like at that inquest.''

He drained the schooner, put it back on the bar, and decided, "Those bullion barons you keep books for wouldn't offer to buy a hole in the ground to set a shithouse on top of. So if Boomer and his pals ain't offering shares, they ain't been handing out ore samples. Meaning somebody must have had some dirt from that claim assayed on their own. I don't know enough about mining law to say whether that's legal or not. It doesn't sound polite. So I can see why nobody who'd make such a sneaky move might want to keep it a private matter. Where did your own mining expert lift the ore samples? From the claim itself or over to the mill owned by members of your syndicate?''

Rothfeld didn't answer. He was staring in horror at his empty shot glass as Longarm went on. "I don't care. They never sent me out this way to regulate mining claims. Don't cut no ice with me whether your outfit is out to skin Boomer Barnes or vice versa. I'm more interested in whether that was really High-grade Hal Diller he brushed with in that taproom than I am about his reasons. Whether they were fighting over pussy or blossom rock won't mean shit if it turns out Boomer had the cuss he was fighting with mixed up with another pain in the ass from Leadville.''

Rothfeld blinked and decided, ''You're surely blessed with a mighty suspicious nature! I only had Boomer Barnes down as a bullshit artist telling whores he's a mining magnate. Why would he point out an innocent man as a killer wanted on a federal warrant?''

Longarm said, ''I doubt he'd do that as a *favor* to the cuss. On the other hand, the man Madam Pearl disarmed and threw out in the cold had drawn on Boomer Barnes for whatever reason. Neither Madam Pearl, who told the local law about the fuss, nor anyone packing their own badge, local or federal, had even laid eyes on High-grade Hal in the flesh. So they had to send for this child.''

Longarm got out a couple of cheroots, saw Rothfeld didn't want one, and thumbnailed a light as he continued. ''When you study on it, not a soul here in Virginia would recognize High-grade Hal for sure on sight but yours truly and Boomer Barnes. After that, nobody but Boomer Barnes says he's certain High-grade Hal Diller has ever been within miles of these parts since he busted out of prison in Kansas. So after we hold that hearing about Jeff Otis, I reckon I'd like to hear some more about High-grade Hal from Boomer Barnes, starting with one fib I've caught him in for certain.''

Chapter 13

It wasn't even noon, and that blamed inquest had been called for three in the afternoon. So Longarm legged it over to Metropolitian Livery Stable #62 to see about some riding. He figured as long as he was there, he'd drop into the gunshop next door and ask about strangers answering to High-grade Hal's description buying Schofield .45's since that excitement at Madam Pearl's.

The young squirt behind the counter repeated what Deputy King Cole had said about that being a silly question. High-grade Hal described a lot like everybody else, and the only reason the Smith & Wesson made to U.S. Army Ordnance specs wasn't as famous as the mythical "Colt .45" was that it took longer to set in type.

Colt's Patent Firearms Manufacturing Company of Hartford, Connecticut, would chamber most any weapon it made in any caliber you liked. So most any Colt six-gun made since the Navy .36 and Army .44 discontinued in '72 could be a "Colt .45," unless it was the Model '73 *marketed* as a .44 "Frontier Model." The same reliable single-action top-strap revolver was sold as the "Peacemaker" when chambered .45-caliber. Longarm and many other serious gun packers favored the more expensive but far more serious Colt double-action Model '78, modified and improved over the first double-actions of '77 and chambered .38, .41, .44, or .45. Sales reps and advertising writers were prone to declare this weapon the Double Action Army, which seemed reasonable, or, wrongly, the Frontier, Thunderer, or even Lightning, which was always a .38. Bewildered newspaper reporters tended to issue a "Colt .45" to anybody taking any part in any gunfight and to hell with it.

But serious shootists from the James boys to Buffalo Bill packed a "Schofield," which was as much a state of mind as a particular brand of side arm.

It usually meant the Smith & Wesson M3 of '71, brought up to those Ordnance specs of the Brothers Schofield, although Remington and even Colt made "Schofields" on special order.

General George Schofield had been made the head of Army Ordnance after the War Between the States. He'd tested and recommended an early version of the S&W M3 to his kid brother, a major with the 10th Cavalry at Fort Leavenworth. So it was no wonder High-grade Hal Diller had been converted to that weapon during his stay at Jefferson Barracks, which was now a federal prison guarded by gents packing surplus army six-guns.

Smith & Wesson had bought Rollin White's 1855 patent for a one-piece extruded metal cartridge to put out their first underpowered Model #1 .22-caliber. Hardly anybody wanted it. They put out the M2 as a .32, and started getting somewhere with the M3 chambered from .41 to .44.

Young Major Schofield ordered some out of his own pocket, and suggested some changes that made the finished product a fast-loading break-open six-gun chambered for .45 Center Fire Shorts at a market price of $14.25 apiece, and that was how come James Butler Hickok had been packing those Schofields instead of "Colt .45's" the day he'd died in Deadwood.

The army had ordered the same model by the thousands. The Czar of All the Russians and even Queeen Victoria had Smith & Wesson cranking out special orders of the same basic weapon.

So that gunshop squirt allowed, and Longarm reluctantly

agreed, that he was only wasting both their time asking about an average-looking son of a bitch in the market for a gun you could buy for five bucks secondhand. Or from most any cowhand packing one for a few dollars more.

Longarm went next door to the livery to look over the riding stock they had for hire. The halfbreed hostler offered him a bargain on a runty fourteen-hands paint mare they called Gimpy.

As Longarm could see, she wasn't really lame. She had one off hind fetlock and hoof mismatched with the other three. So they called her Gimpy and hired her out for two bits a day under your own saddle.

Longarm saddled Gimpy with his McClellan from the tack room, and rode her around the paddock a couple of times to prove he'd been right about that one white fetlock and pink hoof.

For reasons even Professor Darwin couldn't explain, a horse of any color tended to have matching hooves. Even a paint was inclined to have either four white stockings and pale hooves or four dark. Nobody knew why or what this meant. But few riders would set out on a long market drive aboard a bronc with hooves that "didn't look right."

But Longarm couldn't afford to keep a regular mount for occasional riding, seeing he spent so much time around the Denver Federal Building and the nearby Parthenon Saloon on his own two feet. So he'd ridden far more short-term mounts than some, and so far had found it was true you couldn't judge a horse by its color.

But superstitions tended to linger as an aftertaste to common sense, and so as they rode north, Longarm told the paint mare, "Just carry me and this Winchester as far as that new strike claimed by Boomer Barnes and we'll have you home before three."

Gimpy didn't seem to mind as he trotted her out of the business district and through the exotic smells of Chinatown to the north. Chinamen were inclined not to look at regular Americans, even when the latter stared at them and made fun

99

of their pigtails and odd outfits. Longarm was too polite to stare at anybody rudely. But he kept an eye open for any clean-looking noodle joint without a chop suey sign over the door. A waitress gal at the Golden Dragon in Denver had warned him about what the sons of Han threw together as chop suey, which meant something like begger's hash and had no particular formula. She'd told him chop suey had been invented in desperation out California way by a Chinese cook with a mob of forty-niners to feed and nothing but odds and ends left to work with. She'd showed him a swell Oriental position in bed as well, come to study on it.

So he studied on it, wondering how Red Robin might like it as he rode on, having recovered entirely from that unexpected bout with Madam Pearl.

When he got out past a pig farm north of Chinatown, he could see John Hereford's lumber flume striding along a higher contour line on its braced timber legs. Digging metal out of the Sierra Nevada sure used a lot of its trees.

He'd asked directions at the livery. So he knew the claim he aimed to visit had been staked higher up, and when he came upon a footpath leading higher than the coach road at an easy angle, he reined Gimpy to follow it up under the lumber flume. He could tell there was water running above them from the humming of the timbers they passed between, although the V-shaped aqueduct above them didn't seem to be leaking worth mentioning. John Hereford hadn't stinted on stout pine and skilled woodworking. You didn't have to when you had a whole forest of free trees to work with. That Mexican tax on mined bullion did seem a tad steep to Longarm, but some mining magnates north of the border had sure made a lot of friends in Washington. Under the Homestead Act of '63, you had to take good care of the land you claimed and pay taxes on it after you proved your claim. But under the more recent state and federal mining acts, you got to have more fun. Every time somebody objected to what the mine interests were up to, they had their pals in Washington pass another law allowing them to do it. Longarm was glad they'd only sent him after a mining camp asshole who killed folks right out.

The path they'd followed up from the coach road petered out at an abandonded claim where a twenty-foot try-hole still stared open at the sky though all the shacks and supplies had been salvaged. They rode on with that lumber flume down the slope from them, past other try-holes and scattered piles of trash. A flicker of movement caught Longarm's eye, and he glanced over to see a big squared timber of sugar pine whipping on down that flume. He was just as glad he wasn't riding it. He could see how that reporter had gauged the speed of that current at over a hundred miles an hour although, in truth, it was more like thirty. But falling off that tall skinny flume at thirty miles an hour would likely kill you just as dead.

He spied the four white ribbons fluttering in the breeze from long poles around the clutter of tents, supply stacks, and spoil piles of what had to be the claim he was looking for.

To begin with, it was being worked. After that, a lean and hungry-looking cuss with a sawed-off double-barrel Parker stepped around one corner of the army perimeter tent set up just clear of the spoil pile to call out, "That's close enough, stranger! Ride around and we'll both feel better about it."

Longarm rode toward him, calling back, "Blow me out of this saddle and I'll never speak to you again. But I'm the law and you'll be in a whole lot of trouble."

Then the familiar figure of the older and stockier Boomer Barnes came around the other side of the tent to say something to his sidekick Longarm couldn't make out, before he yelled more jovially, "Come on in and have some coffee. Have some beans if you can stand the thought. We were just fixing to knock off for dinner, such as we can afford."

Longarm rode in and dismounted, to be introduced to the shotgun-toter called Slim and another aptly named kid called Porky. Neither face rang any bells as Longarm ran them through his mental file on federal wants.

Slim moved off to put his Parker down across some dynamite crates, as Longarm tethered Gimpy to a wheelbarrow and followed the other two into the tent, where, sure enough, someone had set up tin plates and cups atop an old army map table.

Neither the beans nor the coffee warming on the small scrapwood fire out front smelled appealing. But Longarm allowed he'd try some of their coffee to be polite.

The cup Slim served him as he sat at the table wasn't as bad as it smelled. Campfire coffee seldom was. The aroma of woodsmoke and coffee beans just didn't blend worth a damn.

As the three miners dug in, Longarm waited to be asked what he was doing there. Boomer Barnes tried to hold out until he'd finished his beans. But he was only half through when he soberly allowed he thought they'd about covered everything about his dustup with High-grade Hal at Madam Pearl's.

Longarm said they could talk about it later on alone.

Barnes said, "I have no secrets from Slim and Porky. The boys are my pards. We're working this claim on even shares. That way I get more work out of them."

Neither younger man laughed. The fat boy called Porky shot his older mentor a dirty look and muttered, "That's for sure. I wish *I* was such a fucking genius!"

Boomer Barnes never batted an eye as he replied, "Go strike you own color and you'll find plenty as willing to work it on my generous terms. If you don't like 'em, go work for day wages in the Comstock, sonny."

Porky said, "I would if they was hiring. I sure as shit ain't making three dollars a day up here with you all!"

Longarm hadn't ridden all this way to listen to labor disputes. He sipped some coffee, lowered the tin cup, and quietly said, "Madam Pearl told me you told her you were a married man, Boomer."

The older sourdough smiled ruefully and replied, "I used to marry up when I was young and foolish. Gave it up when I noticed it don't matter whether you've put a ring on her finger or a new dress around her single form, as long as you have the money to spend on her. Married or single, no woman has no respect for a man with no money and vice versa!''

Slim leaned back in his folding camp chair to wail off tune:

I ain't got much use for no woman!
A true one won't never be found!
They'll all stick with a man when he's winning,
And laugh in his face when he's down!

Porky said, ''Amen. I can't afford Madam Pearl's on what I've been making here. The true love I have been seeing wants three dollars for three ways, and I suspect the ugly old bawd really hates it.''

Boomer Barnes smiled fondly and said, ''Miss Joyce says I ain't like her other gentlemen callers. Somebody told her I owned my own mine. I'll give you three guesses who that was.''

Longarm insisted, ''The first time I asked Madam Pearl about that taproom argument you'd had with High-grade Hal, she said she didn't aim to tell me who he'd been fighting with because he, meaning you, was a respectable married man when he wasn't fighting over whores in her taproom. When I insisted, she said she'd see if you'd be willing to talk to me. So I came back later and sure enough, you'd told her you would and you did. So where's this wife Madam Pearl said you wanted to protect, and if there's no such lady, what *were* you trying to hold back on us, old son?''

Boomer Barnes answered flatly, ''Nothing. I never said shit to Madam Pearl or even Miss Joyce about my marital status, which has been single since my last wife run off with a windmill salesman when my last try-hole bottomed out. As to her having to clear it with either of us before we met up last night at her place, all I know is that I'd just rolled off Miss Joyce and hauled my boots back on when Madam Pearl knocked on the door and told us there was a federal lawman who wanted to see me. I met you down in the taproom a few minutes later with not a damned thing to hide. She never said shit about you looking for me earlier. I was up here with these boys all day yesterday. Anybody looking for me only had to ask.''

Longarm insisted, "I did. Her. She said to come back later. Why would she have had any call to lie when she implied you were so shy?''

Barnes shrugged and said, "Ask her. She was the one who lied. I ain't asking you to believe me because you admire my tits. I'll bet you a dollar I can prove she was full of shit when she said she had to get my permit before she introduced me to another lawman!''

Longarm said, "You're on. From where I sit it looks like it's your word against hers.''

Porky muttered, "You'll be sorry.''

Longarm was when Boomer Barnes smiled sweetly and said, "Let's use pure logic and I'll let you decide who's won. The other lawmen out this way sent for you because you'd know High-grade Hal on sight and they'd been told he was in town, right?''

Longarm nodded and Barnes continued. "They knew he was in town because Madam Pearl told them I'd recognized him from Leadville. Did you think a local, state, or federal lawman with the brains to unbutton his pants to piss would send for you on the unsupported word of a whore who'd never known High-grade Hal by that handle? He was staying there as a boarder, telling lies about who he was, up until the night I recognized him. So Lord knows how many lawmen have come out here to talk with me about it before you. You can ask 'em, and I don't accept paper money.''

Longarm smiled sheepishly, and handed over the silver cart-wheel as he marveled, "When you're right you're right. I reckon my natural modesty blinded me to her real motives for luring me back after dark.''

Boomer Barnes said, "Sometimes I suspect Miss Joyce enjoys it more than she lets on. I reckon you want to look over our mine as long as you're out here, right?''

"I was wondering how I'd put that without a search warrant," Longarm replied just as casually.

Chapter 14

Their try-hole ran down into Mount Davidson at a steep angle through uncertain-looking dirt and rocks shored up by guess and by God with not enough scrap lumber. It was barely wide enough for two to work abreast, and a man shorter than Longarm would have had to stoop some under the scantly timbered roof.

Boomer Barnes and Porky led Longarm down to the face, clinging to a hand rope, while Slim guarded the adit above them with that sawed-off Parker. They hadn't worked deep enough to need lamps in the daytime. Boomer said they'd drilled and blasted that morning, and knocked off for dinner to give the fumes some time to clear. Longarm didn't ask about mine ventilation. This glorified rabbit hole was still a far piece from a mine. But he did voice concern about the timbering as he grabbed a post for support on the slope and had it come loose in his hand.

Boomer, just ahead of him, said, "I tried to buy us some Deidesheimer timbers off Consolidated. They wouldn't let us have tailored pine they've been salvaging and selling as firewood from old abandoned galleries. I tried to buy some direct off the Hereford lumber mill up in the high country. Guess what they told me."

Longarm didn't have to. Few businessmen with a natural

105

monopoly had ever volunteered to share it with rivals. He asked, "How come Consolidated Virginia is still buying fresh timbers off Hereford if they've started selling them off?"

Boomer dryly replied, "You did say it was a spell back since you've tried your hand at hardrock mining. You don't use mine timbers over again once they've held the mountain up somewheres else. To begin with, even when they still look sound, used timbers are inclined to lie to you."

Longarm started to ask a dumb question. Then some of it came back to him and he said, "I follow your drift. I'd forgot how old-timers said you could hear timbers moaning low before they commenced to even crackle. Timber that had already given off those first warnings in one part of your mine might not want to talk about shifting weight in yet another, right?"

Boomer said, "Damned right. That's why you see these salvaged house beams and torn-down carpenters' scaffolds in *this* mine. Lots of them salvaged timbers from the Comstock galleries have had all the creaks squoze out of their wood. A pine upright that was put in six feet tall can come out of the mine standing barely five. This ragged-ass wood we've managed to beg, borrow, or steal ain't never been subjected to that kind of pressure. So it ought to give a holler before it lets any rock come down on us."

Porky snorted and chimed in. "Unless a ton of rock wants to peel off *between* them so-called roof beams. We could have regular Deidesheimer framing and some durned *rails* to haul a regular tram along, but Boomer hates Jews too hard to think straight!"

His senior partner flatly said, "Shut up or get off this claim, you windy asshole! Who I might or might not care to do business with is my own damned business, hear?"

Longarm didn't say anything. Sometimes a lawman could find a lot out by just leaving his ears open and his mouth shut.

As they got down to the shattered blossom rock piled against the freshly blasted face, Boomer proved that point by volunteering, "This child never said he hates Jews in particular. He hates *all* those fine-haired sons of bitches who suck around like leeches after a prospector they wouldn't let in their fancy club has taken all the risks and done all the hard work developing a new strike!''

Porky pouted, ''That Jew still made the best offer.''

Boomer bent over to pick up a nondescript lump of rotten quartz that reminded Longarm of that blue French cheese. Boomer held it out to him, saying, ''Put this in your pocket and feel free to carry it down to the smelter. You may make your dollar back with change. They may tell you it ain't worth shit. Gould & Curry don't care who they buy bullion from. Just don't ask them or any other members of the syndicate to give an outsider a break!''

Longarm pocketed the apple-sized ore sample as he stared at the face they'd blasted it from in the uncertain light coming down from outside. Most of it seemed a mottled mix of the busted-up granite set in clay that you'd expect digging anywhere on Mount Davidson that deep. He'd read somewhere how granite formed deep in the earth under pressure, and tended to spall or break apart naturally once it found itself under less strain. Groundwater seeping through cracks in granite slowly turned the mostly feldspar bedrock into clay. Longarm saw a darker ink blob of the softer blossom rock centered in the freshly drilled and blasted face.

As if he read minds, Boomer Barnes pointed at it with his chin to say, ''Fifty dollars a ton, more or less. Metallic salts in weathered quartz. The way I read her, she bubbled up through a thermal vent from the mother lode many moons ago with the gold, silver, arsenic, and other shit in solution. As the vein solidified, the metal never precipitated even. But it's in there, like raisins in a cake. Mostly silver, as you might expect, but more gold mixed in than you'll find over to the main Comstock Lode.''

Longarm nodded. It was coming back to him. He said, ''You're telling me you don't think this lead bubbled up from the same mother lode as they've been mining up to now.''

Boomer said, ''Don't see how it could. Same mountain. Same colors. But *blended* different. The big bonanza struck as a blossom rock lead back in '59 came bubbling strange from the bowels of the mountain. It stands on end like it was the high end of a sort of silver reef coming straight up out of Hell. But like August Sutro proved by tunneling in under it, the Comstock Lode *bottoms out* less than four thousand feet down."

"Meaning?" Longarm asked.

Barnes said, "Meaning them fine-haired sons of bitches with their fancy books they get to read in club chairs don't know everything! *I* say you don't get something out of nothing. That Comstock Lode never grew by itself like Topsy in *Uncle Tom's Cabin* to become a lump of ore that big with no connections to any damned *source*! If all that bullion-bearing quartz didn't bubble up from bigger lodes below, it must have run in from somewhere *else* to fill a swamping hole in the ground."

Longarm raised a brow and said, "No offense, but the way I hear it, a heap of mining men, fine-haired or hardworking, have searched high and low for color beyond the known boundaries of the Comstock Lode."

The older man said, "They should have looked *sideways*, like me! I don't know whether this lead we're following *away* from the Comstock instead of *towards* it will take us to the source of that big but played-out strike or another source entire. I hope this strike turns out to be another one. The color we've mucked so far assays different. But either way, I mean to make it mine, all mine!"

Then he caught the glare in Porky's eye and added, "Mine and my two junior pards', that is. Have you seen enough? Me and the boys have to get back to work."

Longarm allowed he'd satisfied himself they weren't hiding High-grade Hal Diller from him in their try-hole. So Boomer allowed he'd stay put and start mucking if Porky wanted to see their visitor to the adit.

It wasn't easy, but as they climbed the steep slope together, Longarm refrained from asking the disgruntled Porky any questions. He'd found that possible witnesses who were pissed off at the boss were more likely to talk if you just let them.

So sure enough, when they got to the adit to climb out, blinking in the afternoon sunlight, Porky told Slim, "I'll toss you for which of us gets to stand guard for now and who gets to haul that fucking box of ore up them uneven planks! We could have a regular tram running on tracks with a steam donkey doing all that work if the stubborn old cuss would just listen to that friendly Jew."

Slim said, "There's no such thing as a friendly Jew. He's asking a quarter share for setting on his ass in town whilst we do all the work!"

"With his money!" Porky pointed out, adding in a petulant tone, "He offered to grubstake us generous. Full timbering, a Burleigh air drill to go with them rails and steam donkey, and most of all, better *grub*! A growing boy needs more than biscuits and beans to go with his damned black coffee!"

Slim didn't look at Longarm as he suggested, "Talk to Boomer about it. It ain't for anyone here to say how Boomer runs things on this claim. As to tossing for whose turn it might be to help the old man muck, it's your turn. I mucked last time, and like the Indian chief said, I have spoken!"

Longarm bade them both good afternoon and when neither answered, he told them to go fuck themselves as he untethered his livery mount from their wheelbarrow.

He mounted up and headed back to town, letting Gimpy have her head on the uncertain slope when he saw he still had plenty of time to make that coroner's inquest.

He knew what had happened the night before at Red Robin's hotel. As he rode back to town at a walk, he spent more thought on matters he found more mysterious. The late Jeff Otis hadn't come after him like that on a lark. He'd been a hired gun, hired by somebody to gun a lawman. So he'd tried to set up an excuse in advance by making it appear they were at feud, with the poor reluctant killer forced into a fight he'd never wanted and so on, all the way to the gallows.

It seemed doubtful Otis had been retained as a paid assassin by the murderous High-grade Hal Diller. The man they'd sent a senior deputy to identify had motive, sort of, but neither the means nor opportunity to hire a gunslick from Reno if he was looking for a job and acting that desperate when he got turned down.

Besides, Diller was the sort who liked to do his own killing, even when he could afford to hire guns.

Hardly anyone else on the side of the law could have known the law out this way had sent for him. That meant it had to be somebody more likely than a wanted outlaw to gossip with local lawmen.

Madam Pearl had known local lawmen well enough to gossip about that fuss between Diller and Barnes in her taproom. But it hardly seemed likely she'd have told the law Diller had been hiding out at her whorehouse if they were plotting against lawmen together, and Diller had reason to believe Madam Pearl sort of liked him.

So who had Longarm caught in any recent lies, save for Nat Rothfeld, if Rothfeld was the Jewish backer Barnes and his boys had been talking about back yonder?

It hardly seemed likely they'd been speaking of Meyer Guggenheim, the Swiss-born lace-maker of Hebrew persuasion who'd started to make a name for himself around Leadville as a shrewder grubstaker than old Silver Dollar Tabor. For while Hod Tabor and his formidable Augusta had tended to back most any prospector modestly, Meyer Guggenheim had to be convinced you were on to something before he backed you to the hilt.

Mining was such a gamble there was much to be said for both approaches. The Tabors had bought that salted mine off Chicken Bill and drilled on through into a rich vein through pure shithouse luck, while Guggenheim had paid for the steam pump and expensive plumbing it had taken to drain that flooded high-grade he'd been able to buy for a song. Old Professor Darwin could likely explain why folks of any persuasion heading West had the same restless natures and drives. Whatever the reason, and no matter what they called each other, the Irish and Jews forced to leave their old countries, and not welcomed too warmly in the Eastern states, tended to form a common alliance as Western businessmen. So Nat Rothfeld was hardly the only Jewish grubstaker Boomer Barnes could have turned down. Nat had dismissed Boomer as a small-timer with a big mouth, and old Nat seemed a truthful cuss. But how safe would it be to ask him about other possible investors of the same persuasion when it was still possible the cuss had been fibbing?

But it didn't make much sense for Boomer to refuse any backing from any backer. Cutting a man with a head for figures and deep pockets into an unproven strike would make sense, even when he didn't have his own connections with the big combination that ran the silver game here in Nevada. Buying into a try-hole producing enough color to pay its own way made sense as well, provided the investment was modest and your cut was one quarter. So why would either try to hide such dickerings from a federal lawman, assuming that was all there was to it?

"There's more to it," Longarm told the paint he was riding as she carried him back through Chinatown.

Meanwhile, he had that tedious inquest to sit through before he and good old Red Robin might have at least a quick one before she had to get back to the Crystal Palace. So he returned Gimpy and his saddle to the livery, and legged it on over to the courthouse.

That was where things started to spoil his day for him. Nobody gave him a hard time about gunning Jeff Otis. The gunslick had been a pest somebody should have gunned much earlier, and plenty of witnesses came forward to testify the asshole had been spoiling for a fight with Longarm since before the two of them had arrived in Virginia. The Wells Fargo crew and Miss Lili FitzRoy from the opera company agreed Otis had been the one in the wrong when coming down from Reno. Nat Rothfeld, sitting on the panel, chimed in to back the opera singer, and the coroner said that in that case he was ruling the cause of death was suicide and there was no need to swear in any other witnesses.

Longarm was glad. He hadn't wanted to testify lest they ask questions about him and Red Robin. He'd been more worried about her testimony after he'd noticed she hadn't shown up for the inquest. For ignoring a summons could get a stranger in town in trouble.

But since she was never called to the stand, it never happened, and he lit out for her hotel to see if she was all right as soon as the part-time coroner said the case was closed and they were all free to go get that drink if they cared to.

When he got to Red Robin's hotel they told him she'd left town and left a message for him, if he was Custis Long.

He said he was, tipped the desk clerk two bits, and tore open the envelope to read Red Robin's tender but terse message.

She'd been fired at the Crystal Palace for sassing the night manager and getting involved in a scandal. That was what they called it when a lady had a shootout in her quarters—a scandal. She said she was headed next for Durango, where she had another job lined up, and allowed she'd be thinking of him on the train that evening as she jerked herself off.

He pocketed her sass to dispose of later discreetly as he consulted his watch and softly muttered, "Well, I sure ain't about to catch my wanted man aboard that train with the gal I wanted this evening. But I reckon I'll have me some supper before I jerk off!"

Chapter 15

Red Robin's fancier hotel had a bigger dining room than his own. But Longarm knew if he ate too early he'd wind up too hungry to sleep later on. So as long as he had some time to kill, he scouted up a nearby assay office and sauntered in to ask the old gray owl inside how much that ore sample might be worth.

The old bird behind the counter stared at him and his cheesy lump of blossom rock through glasses thick enough for shot glasses as he said, "We were fixing to close. My old woman has a chicken in the oven. But I can tell that's from the Barnes claim without my blowpipe or the acid test."

Longarm nodded soberly and said, "You're pretty good. How good is this ore?"

The old owl shrugged and said, "Can't say from just looking. Smelt a ton that looks about the same and you ought to wind up with fifty or more, or less—it's been sort of patchy so far."

Longarm said, "That's what they told me. They said this blossom rock ain't the the same as you find wrapped around the Comstock Lode. What do *you* say as an old pro?"

The assay man preened like a wise old owl who'd been complimented by a fighting cock and said, "They were right. I don't know the hows and whys as surely as the professors who write books do. Color seems to be where you find it when you get down to digging in the dirt. But for reasons best known to Mother Nature, Barnes has been mucking a somewhat different formation. A higher percentage of gold but less metal overall. So once you smelt it down to richer ingots, you wind up with about a fifty-a-ton average. Different figures to end up nigh the same answer in the end.''

Longarm ran a thumbnail along his jawline, noting he could use a shave, and said, ''I'm missing something. Consolidated Virginia allows tribute mining of the blossom rock you assay as worth about the same. So why should some bigwig be offering to invest in Boomer's claim if he's only been digging blossom rock a tad richer?''

The expert in mining manners said, ''A tad is a tad and you don't buy a crust of a loaf. They buy the bread. The gut-and-git prospectors skim the easy but limited high-grade and move on, if they're dumb, or sell out to the bigger outfits who can invest enough to mine the bigger mother lodes. You can afford to settle for less than tads a ton as soon as you get tons and tons on their way to the smelter. Do you want me to assay this particular sample for you in the morning?''

Longarm shook his head and said, ''I'll take your word Boomer's claim sounds like a sensible investment. That's likely why he's turned down at least one offer to grubstake him for a quarter share.''

The owlish assay man said he'd like to see some solid quartz under all that blossom rock, but agreed grubstakers had gotten rich betting against greater odds. So they shook on it, and Longarm left the ore sample with any proceeds going to the old-timer's favorite charity or a good cigar, depending.

At the Western Union down the way, he found Billy Vail had wired him orders to keep up the good work and thrown in a few suggestions. He put the telegram away to read over more carefully later, and got off his own progress report, which didn't take up half the space.

Coming out of the Western Union, he met the federal lawman they called King Cole coming along the walk. So they ducked into the next saloon down to compare notes on High-grade Hal.

They ordered draft at the bar, seeing they were both on duty that afternoon. King Cole said he and his own boys had scouted other whorehouses, boarding houses, and joss houses over in Chinatown in the hopes of finding somebody, anybody, who might have noticed a new face in their neck of the woods. Longarm agreed it was a pisser when you had to describe such an average-sounding suspect to possible witnesses who got to see so many average gents in passing.

He said, "Your field of fire makes sense, though. After Madam Pearl threw him out of her place, he must have wound up someplace else. Have you gents considered what that fuss he had with Boomer Barnes might say about the state of his pocket jingle?"

King Cole sipped some suds, nodded, and said, "Sure we have. A man who throws down on you when you refuse him a job must need a job sort of serious. Madam Pearl had been charging him an arm and a leg for more than the usual comforts of home. There haven't been any serious hold ups here in Virginia since Madam Pearl says she first laid eyes on the owlhoot rider. So he arrived with ill-gotten gains, spent a heap of 'em, and meant it when he told Boomer he wanted a job in his mine."

Longarm said, "I rode out to Boomer's claim earlier today. Boomer ain't working what I'd call a mine. So he would have been polite turning down a hardrock man with an honest rep. Since Diller don't seem to be out robbing folks, he's likely found some other job. That might narrow things down if we were to ask around about new hands hired within the time since Madam Pearl took Diller's six-gun away and threw him out on his ear."

King Cole nodded, but said, "That would still leave any of our riders walking on eggs if some boss told them he *had* such a suspect on the premises. You're the only lawman in town who'd know Diller on sight, and it ain't polite to slap leather on the wrong man!"

Longarm patted the folded telgram in his coat pocket and suggested, "Not recognizing faces works both ways. Why not tell your deputies to just play dumb when and if they come across a recently hired hand who fits that nondescript description. I'd be proud to come around with them at quitting time for a look at the bird as he leaves for the day, and even better, Marshal Vail just wired that they're sending us some federal turnkeys from Jefferson Barracks. It'll take 'em a few days to get here from Leavenworth, but once they do, High-grade Hal could be in a whole heap of trouble. None of those Kansas hands are likely to thank him for killing one of their own."

King Cole said, "We could sure use some help with the plain-looking son of a bitch. There's over ten thousand faces to look at here in Virginia, even after all them layoffs, and as in the case with that Schofield .45 Madam Pearl took away from him, you get a considerable innocent turnover in a town this size when it comes to gunshops, boardinghouses, and day labor."

Longarm allowed he'd keep his own eyes peeled as he moved about as much as he could. He said, "I've found on other missions that taking an interest in local matters tends to keep a man on his feet with his eyes and mind open. Just keeping an eye on the last known address of a want whilst you stare like hell at the few faces in sight can put you to sleep whilst you think you're doing your job. Have you ever mislaid something and wasted the better part of an hour trying to remember where you put it as you rummage high and low?"

King Cole said, "Don't try and teach your granny to suck eggs. We've all done that. The best way to find your missing keys or favorite pipe is to just get on with your chores and let 'em turn up natural, where they've been all the time. So what local matters are you working on here in Virginia—that banshee hunt they're having later tonight?"

Longarm started to shake his head, shrugged, and said, "Tell me more about it before I have to answer."

The federal lawman said, "Midnight, to give the banshee

116

time to think she has all them dark empty galleries to herself. They're clearing the Consolidated mines entire at the regular quitting time this evening. Then, on the stroke of twelve, the limelights they're borrowing off John Piper from his opera house blaze their beams through as many main galleries as they can manage and the company police start a sweep in a sort of vertical skirmish line, north to south, with other company police and volunteer guns laying in ambush near the south ends and working hoists. They asked if we wanted in on it. Our marshal told 'em he'd have to study on it. High-grade Hal is famous for stealing high-grade ore from mines. But the boss just can't imagine him singing so high, even if he had a sensible motive.''

Longarm grimaced and said, "If anyone could figure out the *motive* behind all that spooky screaming, they'd have that banshee caught in no time. He, she, or it has to be either a noisy lunatic or somebody more reasonable with reasons that elude this child entirely!''

They finished their beer and agreed they might or might not meet at midnight for that banshee hunt if nothing more interesting turned up later on that evening.

By then it was getting late enough to consider that supper. Longarm went back to Red Robin's hotel and followed the tempting odors of high-toned cooking through the archway off the lobby to see that, just as *he* had, others had suspected they might serve tolerable grub there.

You weren't allowed to just tear in and grab yourself a table in a first-class restaurant. So Longarm had to stand with his hat in his hand until a Mexican with a French accent and a claw-hammer coat came over to lead him to a seat at one of their linen-covered tables. As Longarm waited, he spied that opera tenor, Santini, over against the rosy wallpaper, having supper with that brown-haired gal from his outfit that Longarm sort of liked. The good ones always seemed to be taken. That was the only argument for settling down that made a lick of sense to Longarm. He'd been tempted now and again to get up from the game with his winnings when he'd won somebody really likeable. The trick was to hang in there undecided until they started to nag a man about getting a safer job or at least giving up those disgusting three-for-a-nickel cheroots.

That often took place even before going to bed with the same woman night after night began to feel like a chore. Old Santini looked like a sensible young cuss. Longarm idly wondered how long it might be before the two of them broke up, and whether anything that nice would like a shoulder to cry on once they did.

The Mexican maitre d' came over to ask if he was Marshal Long. Longarm allowed he was only a deputy, but owned up to the rest. So the headwaiter led him through the crowded tables in a zigzag as Longarm idly wondered what had given the jasper the notion that he'd made a reservation.

Then he saw they were headed for a corner table where two familiar figures were already seated—and not bad figures they were that evening, in low-cut summer frocks. From their cleavage up they were those two opera gals he'd put to bed the night before, Lili FitzRoy and auburn-haired Flora Livingston. The Mexican pulled out a chair for him, so Longarm knew they'd extended the invitation.

He howdied the ladies and sat down with his hat in his lap to read the menu the maitre d' handed him. The two opera gals were already half done with their soup. Longarm allowed he'd skip that course lest they leave him in the dust. As he looked the menu over, he was already having second thoughts about feeding himself there. He was going to have to offer to pay for them, at least, and if they ordered soup to nuts, he'd be lucky to get out of there spending less than five dollars.

When they said they'd have fried chicken with asparagus and spuds next, Longarm said he'd have the same, even though he'd have gone for the more costly porterhouse with spuds, and to hell with the rabbit food, if he'd been dining alone.

As if she'd read his mind, Lili said it was her treat, shyly adding, "It's the least I can do for such a gallant swain. I owe you for defending me against that brute they were talking about this afternoon at his inquest, and I don't know what came over me last night after just a few tiny drinks!''

Her auburn-haired pal chimed in. "We were so worried you'd involve poor Lili in a scandal when you testified about that duel upstairs.''

Longarm blinked and asked, "How come? I never got to testify this afternoon. But if I had, I can't think of anything scandalous I might have said about any of you opera gals, no offense. That hired gun and me weren't fighting a duel. He was out to gun me personal. I'd said good night to you ladies on another floor before I even noticed he was after me.''

The two of them exchanged glances. Lili smiled across the table and confessed, "We were both a tad confused about that when we woke up fully dressed and just a tad hung over. Some men might have taken . . . advantage of two sillies who'd imbibed unwisely but all too well.''

Flora smiled sort of dirty and murmured, "Fess up. Weren't you at least sort of tempted?''

Longarm smiled indulgently and replied in an easy tone, "Sure I was. Do I look sickly or unmanly? Sometimes I find it tempting when I see someone's left money on the counter that the waitress hasn't seen there yet. That don't mean I ought to take advantage of her.''

As the soup bowls were cleared away, Longarm turned back to the small brunette to say, "Seeing you feel you owe me, Miss Lili, can I ask you a personal question?''

She fluttered her lashes and said she hoped it wasn't *too* personal.

He said, "Call it nosy. They pay me to be nosy about everything and everybody as I wend my way through this wicked world. So I couldn't help wondering how come the two of us first met aboard that Wells Fargo coach from Reno yesterday.''

It was her turn to look surprised. She said, "I told you at the time. I was on my way here from Reno. What's so mysterious about that?''

"Why we met aboard a coach on my way here,'' Longarm

insisted. "In the natural order of fate, you should have been here already with all the rest of your company. They told me at the opera house your outfit had replaced the bunch putting on *The Barber of Seville*. They never said your bunch was on its way. They said they were in town. All of 'em but *you* were. You don't have to tell me what you were doing up in Reno if you don't want to. I just thought I'd ask."

Lili hesitated, blushed demurely, and confessed, "All right, if you must know, I was seeing a . . . friend off aboard an eastbound train. We drove up to Reno with another couple in their private carriage. I had to take the coach back when it developed they intended to stay in Reno a while."

"Her husband's in Washington to argue about the silver standard," Flora explained archly.

Lili said, "Flora, for heaven's sake . . ."

The other opera gal laughed and said, "You're not the one having an affair with that handsome cattleman, you poor thing. Tell this lawman what you were doing aboard that coach before he arrests us both as road agents!"

Longarm said he wasn't interested in such gossip as the waiter came to serve their main entrees. As he did so, Flora asked, "Not interested? Don't you mean it doesn't sound like a federal offense? I thought all of us were *interested* in such matters, Custis."

He let that go past him. Lili hushed her with a look, and waited till the waiter left before she murmured, "Custis isn't like that. He had the two of us at his mercy across my *bed* last night, if he hadn't been such a gentleman of the old school."

Flora began to cut with her fork in her left hand, fancy old-country-style, as she impishly asked, "Old school or getting old?"

Longarm started to eat American-style as he sighed and said, "Call me a sissy and let's say no more about last night. You gals had had too much, and I reckon I hadn't had enough to take advantage of the situation. Just see that it never happens again."

Lili fluttered her lashes at her chicken and asparagus. But Flora asked, "Is that a promise? Are you warning us or making an offer?"

Longarm washed some grub down with the ice water provided, and soberly replied, "Both. Last night I had more lady friends in town than I have right now, and I had to consider that the two of you had drunk too much by accident. So let's lay out some rules on the defense claims of hard liquor under Anglo-American common law."

"Oh, do we have to?" pouted the frisky Flora.

Longarm said, "We do. I know some Texas folks who trade with the Far East out of Galveston. This Japanese gent they have working for them tells me that under Japanese jurisprudence you can claim you were too drunk to know right from wrong, the same as you can plead insanity in an American court. This is likely why Japanese drunks are reputed to be the meanest drunks on Earth. One of those gents from Old Nippon can butcher his wife and kids along with the next-door neighbors and plead he was just drunk at the time. So whenever a mean drunk starts to mutter to himself in a Japanese saloon, the rest of the patrons tend to run for their lives, unless somebody wants to just kill the pest and brag that they were drunker. My point is that you're allowed to do most anything you want and blame it on your booze in Dai Nippon. That's what they call the place—Dai Nippon."

Flora said, "We *thought* you were a man of the world. What has the law to say about getting crazy drunk here in Virginia City?"

He said, "A few years back in this very town a lady called Miss Julia Bulette was strangled by a mean drunk one night. At his trial he swore he'd been so drunk he didn't remember doing it. The judge said it didn't matter. He'd known what he was doing when he started drinking. When you know you're a mean drunk, or any other sort of drunk, it's up to you not to drink, or be prepared to accept the consequences once you sober up."

It was little Lili who softly murmured, "I think he's warning us not to get drunk around him a second time unless we mean it."

To which Flora gamely replied, "Sounds that way to me too. I can hardly wait."

Chapter 16

In the end it cost Longarm more than five dollars to settle the tab because that brown-haired gal he'd liked best, Miss Miranda, came to join them for coffee and dessert for some reason.

Longarm liked her less, and savvied her reason better, when she sat down uninvited and muttered "Men!" as if he was one of the gals.

But Longarm forgave the bunch of them once they got to jawing about Enzio Santini and some "spear carriers" from Virginia City fixing to go banshee hunting with the lighting crew and some stagehands from Piper's Opera House. He hadn't even thought about spear carriers, and so now he could likely get away with charging all this fancy grub to entertaining federal informants.

He said, "When I was on tour with the Divine Sarah, she called the extra help she picked up along the way spear carriers. I forgot to ask her why she called them that."

Miranda said, "It saves a lot of money when an opera company only pays the travel expenses of the singing cast. Each opera house along the way has its own stage crew to help with the lighting, scenery, and so forth. For crowd scenes on stage, it's cheap and easy to hire some of the local talent. There's always a drama club or, in a pinch, poetic stable hands and housemaids who always wanted to appear in costume with or without a spear to carry. Sometimes our manager can get them to carry a spear for nothing.''

Longarm nodded and said, ''It's all coming back to me now. A local talent with a steady job might not apply for the position with you all, no offense. But some old boy without any visible means might find the notion amusing. Getting paid to hide out in plain sight behind stage makeup and an opera costume has cleaning out stables beat by miles. So I reckon I'll tag along with the rest of 'em come midnight. No telling how much extra help the company police might take on by the hour either, as soon as you consider the day shift ought to be sound asleep at that hour.''

The brown-haired Miranda swore under her breath and said, ''You too? What is it about you men that makes you dash off to fights you have no business in? I lost two uncles and an older brother in the war, fighting to save our Southern way of life, and not owning one slave between the three of them! My brother, Matt, died at Shiloh a few days after his seventeenth birthday. Neither of my uncles had been out on their own long enough to know what anyone was fighting for, and now that damned Enzio wants to fight ghosts in a silver mine! For heaven's sake, he's a *tenor,* not a gunfighter!''

She stared owlishly at Longarm and added, ''You're a man. Tell me what it is I seem to be overlooking here!''

Longarm shrugged and said, ''I reckon you've summed it up, ma'am. By your own definition, I'm a man and you ain't. Not a man in a hundred could tell us why ladies are so interested in the latest fashions out of Paris, France, or why it's so important to invite folks you hate to a fancy ball you could barely afford if you only invited your pals. So by the same token, not a woman in a hundred could say why men care less about their appearance, won't drink with other men they detest, or perk up at the distant sounds of battle.''

He sipped the last of his dessert coffee and added, ''As for myself alone this evening, I won't be as anxious to catch that screaming gal over to the Comstock works as I'll be about other men offering to help the company police. I've yet to ask what they're paying by way of posse money. It's usually a dollar for any part of a day. You say old Enzio headed over to the opera house to posse up with his own pals first?''

Miranda said, ''That's what he just said. I told him not to pester me when he gets back after midnight if he finds my company so tiresome! I'm sure you know your way to Piper's Opera House, Deputy Longarm. I'm going upstairs to wash my hair and get in bed with *Ben Hur*.''

''Ben *who*?'' asked Flora Livingston with a roguish smile.

Longarm said, ''*Ben Hur* is that new novel by Governor Lew Wallace of New Mexico Territory, Miss Flora. I can see why Miss Miranda would want to start it early in the evening. It's been published in two volumes, and either one of 'em would take longer to read than *Tom Sawyer* with pages left over.''

''Have you read it?'' Miranda asked.

He said, ''Yes, ma'am. I'd tell you who wins that big chariot race, but that might spoil the fun for you. They say the author visited the Holy Land betwixt serving as a general during the war and cleaning up New Mexico more recently. I reckon he must have. He put stuff in *Ben Hur* I never read in the Good Book.''

Then he signaled their waiter he was ready for the tally. He had to stand up and wait for it when Miranda and Lili got up from the table together. Not a man in a hundred could explain why women went to the shithouse in pairs, come to study on *that*. Longarm and most of the men he knew preferred to be alone with such thoughts. As the waiter and two gals left, Longarm saw the auburn-haired Flora was still sitting there. He sat back down and said, ''I didn't know you wanted more, ma'am. I can call that waiter back if you do.''

She smiled across the table at him and said, ''I thought I'd see you over to the opera house. You might have trouble getting inside on your own at this hour.''

It was just about sundown, and they knew Longarm backstage at Piper's Opera House. But he felt no call to say a dumb thing like that with at least four hours to kill before midnight. So he helped her to her feet and let their waiter keep such change as they might have coming. From the smile they got on the way out, he knew he'd figured the tip about right.

The opera folks were staying at that hotel because it was close to Piper's Opera House. So Longarm offered Flora his elbow, and they were there in next to no time after a pleasant stroll in the Sierra Nevada gloaming, under wispy golden clouds against a lavender sky.

The doorman knew them both, but Flora seemed to feel she'd gotten him inside as they entered to find it brighter backstage than outside.

Longarm could see nobody in the considerable crowd was High-grade Hal because Mr. Edison's newfangled lightbulbs couldn't hold a candle, literally, to the old-fashioned theatrical limelights. They had six of them spread out across the stage behind the asbestos curtain, although only one was lit at the moment, but one was enough as it bounced its harsh beam off the bricks of the back wall.

Each limelight stood on its own rolling stand in a tin box the size of a trunk. Longarm knew how the one they had going was casting all that light. So he didn't crowd in. The hand who operated it for the opera house was explaining to lawmen and mine workers who'd clustered around him how the already bright flame of a hand-pumped oil lamp licked at a bigger lump of white-hot limestone to shoot its much brighter glow through a square flat Fresnel lens like they had in lighthouses. It wasn't for Longarm to say. But he'd have had that beam aimed at the far back of the audience seats if it had been. There was just no saying how far a limelight meant for an opera house might shine in a silver mine.

Enzio Santini had been talking to John Piper himself and a shorter gent Flora identified as their company manager. When Santini spotted them, he came over to nod at Flora and shake with Longarm.

He said, "I've offered to work one of those limelights for the big midnight banshee hunt. The outfit I had on in that Sutro tunnel is still in the cleaners. What are you going to wear tonight?''

Longarm said, "Got some jeans and a denim shirt in my saddlebags. If I was in your shoes I'd borrow some bib overalls off one of your stagehands. With mayhaps an undershirt. It's going to be hotter in the higher galleries than it was down there in the Sutro.''

Santini said he'd heard as much, and asked in a more concerned tone whether Longarm thought they had enough limelights to really matter.

Longarm grimaced and said, "Nope. But two moving in along the top, with two more just above the Sutro and the other two spaced out at the one- and two-thousand-foot levels, ought to cut off some scampers, and the skirmishers above and below the serious beams will have bull's-eye lanterns that grope the dark better than your average blind man's cane.''

Santini thanked Longarm for explaining, and told Flora he had to dash back to their hotel and see if he could calm his Miranda down.

She told him lightly not to bet on it. She didn't seem as worried as Santini about Santini's love life. As the tenor left, she laughed and confided to Longarm, "That's not what they've been fighting about, you know.''

Longarm allowed such fussing was neither a federal offense nor any of his own beeswax. But the auburn-haired soprano said, "He's tired of life on the road and wants to invest some money and let others work for him. Miranda likes to travel and still has hopes of someday singing at La Scala. That's in Italy, where a singer really has to know the ropes.''

Longarm said he'd read that someplace. He said, "I think it was at that picky opera house that the audience kept clapping for this one famous tenor to come back out and sing another chorus, until he held up a hand all out of breath and begged for mercy. But they just yelled back that they expected him to go on singing that same song until he got it right.''

Flora made a wry face and said, "That's an old joke. Don't ever tell it to Miranda. She takes her career seriously. Let's go up those stairs. I want to show you something."

Longarm was game. They weren't fixing to go banshee hunting for hours. But he was still confused when, once she'd led him along a platform that smelled of greaspaint, sweat, and rope dust, he found himself in a dark room with her.

As he thumbed a match head and put it to the wall lamp nearest the door, he saw they were in a small dressing room with a big mirror that reflected a fair-sized sofa bed tucked between steamer trunks against the wall across from the makeup counter.

Flora said, "Lili and me share this dressing room. She's the only one who has another key. That door has an automatic latch unless we set it to open."

Longarm nodded soberly and said, "I was here at Piper's Opera House with Miss Sarah Bernhardt's outfit, Miss Flora. They explained why you ladies feel safer napping between shows behind a locked door."

She moved closer and smiled archly up at him as she confided, "You'd be surprised what goes on behind locked doors backstage. It's a long-established tradition that nobody notices anything that isn't taking place on the stage, see?"

Longarm nodded soberly and said, "Learned not to see while I was touring with that French theatrical outfit. French gals running for a costume change are inclined to shuck their duds along the way in front of the Lord and any stagehands in the way. Nobody working backstage seems to notice. Indians who live in tipis act the same way. When you can't secure privacy behind solid walls, you have to sort of agree not to peek. The Lakota allow that a man has the right to kill another man he catches messing with his wives without his permission. But it's up to him to catch him. Nobody else ever seems to notice."

She suddenly stamped a foot and blazed, "I *thought* you might be part Indian, you tall, dark, and handsome oaf! What's the matter with us? Do you really favor Lili as much as she boasts? Do you want me to fix the two of you shy young things up?"

Longarm blinked down at her and replied, "Lord have mercy, I never said I liked Miss Lili better than anybody else. Whatever gave either one of you that notion?"

Flora picked some imaginary lint from his brown tweed vest as she said, "I thought she was laying it on until last night. But that awful Jeff Otis pestered her aboard the coach from Reno, and then when he was after her at our hotel last night—"

Longarm laughed. "That hired gun wasn't after *her*. He was after *me*. I'm still working on why."

He noticed her eyes were green flecked with gold as she stared up at him and demanded, "At our hotel? I thought you were staying over at the Taylor Hotel. Why were you waiting for us in the lobby of our own hotel if you were neither courting nor guarding Lili as she says?"

Longarm started to say he'd gone there to bang Red Robin, but that was no way to talk behind a lady's back. So seeing Flora expected some damned answer, he just reached out to haul her in and kiss her.

From the way she kissed back he suspected she'd been hoping he might, and what the hell, he had the time and she'd as much as led him by the dong to the place.

It didn't take much spit-swapping, and she never protested she just wasn't that sort of a girl before he had her over on that sofa bed and she was showing him what kind of a girl she was, on top, with all her duds off, save for her black lisle stockings, high-button shoes, and the black velvet band around her ivory throat.

Longarm still had his undershirt on because she'd shoved him on his back to fork a leg across him and grab the saddle-horn while his other duds and gunbelt were still fluttering to the floor.

He didn't mind. No mere virgin could have clasped his organ-grinder that tightly as she moved up and down it with one foot on the floor and the other braced in the crack between the covers and the wall. She had some of her weight braced on her locked elbows with her palms spread on his chest. She

129

said she liked men with hair on their chest. He congratulated her on having such smooth bare tits as they rolled up and down between her braced upper arms. Then she wanted to kiss some more, and it got a tad awkward to keep it all the way in with her all the way down against him. So he rolled her over on her back to finish right with an elbow tucked under each of her upraised black-sheathed knees.

They'd found another swell position in front of that mirror, with him seated in a bentwood chair with her facing him, a foot on the floor to either side of the chair's back legs, when there came the sound of a key turning in the lock and Longarm was suddenly, painfully, aware that neither his derringer nor .44-40 were within reach.

Then it was Lili FitzRoy's turn to stamp a foot as she stood there in the doorway, mad as a wet hen, protesting, "That's not fair! I saw him first and he likes me best!"

To which Flora demurely replied, not missing a stroke as she went right on fucking, "Oh, for heaven's sake, come in and shut that damned door! Nobody said he didn't like you, and there's enough here for everyone if we don't tell Miranda!"

Chapter 17

Lili ducked outside and slammed the door as her chum kept right on bumping and grinding. Longarm groaned that he wanted to move back to the sofa bed because he was almost there again and found their current position a tad awkward. But Flora husked, "I'm coming! Save some for poor little Lili!"

Before Longarm could ask a dumb question, the petite brunette came back in, slammed the door behind her, and sobbed, "Well, maybe just this once, seeing he's so excited. But I don't know how I'll ever be able to explain this next Saturday at Confession!"

Flora shuddered all over, kissed Longarm fondly, and allowed there was much to be said for being Scotch Presbyterian. As she sat limply throbbing around Longarm's renewed lust, she added, "We don't *get* to confess our sins and ask forgiveness. Cut a deck of cards or dance with one boy at the Grange hall and you're doomed to hellfire and damnation. So you may as well drink and fuck all you like while there's still the time. Why don't you give some of this to Lili while it's still hard?"

They both laughed when Longarm dryly remarked she'd have to give it back to him first. As she bit down fondly, then slid off, he saw Lili had peeled off her own summer frock and seemed to be awaiting his pleasure on her hands and knees atop that sofa bed with her face turned to the wall. Her nicely formed but smaller rump was blushing too.

So Longarm didn't say anything sassy as he rose stiffly from the chair, still stiff enough where it counted, and moved quietly over to gently take a hipbone in either hand, put one knee up between her mesh-covered calves, and let it see if it could find its way.

She demurely reached down with one hand to guide it between the soft fuzzy gates of Paradise, and as ever, he was astonished but not dismayed by how different two empty spaces with warm willing women wrapped around them could feel. Lili flinched, and if anything tried to dilate her wet innards away from his probing shaft as it entered her, and then entered her some more.

Burying her face in the covers with her rump thrust even higher, she protested, "It's so big and all sticky with another woman's juices, and how can you treat me this way, you brute?"

To which Longarm could only reply, "Aw, it ain't so hard when a gal puts it in for you. Would you rather I took it out?"

"He knows where he can put it!" bragged Flora as she watched them while seated in that chair and idly strumming her own banjo.

Lili sobbed, "It's too late. I'm lost, lost to my own warm nature, and I've always *tried* to be a good girl!"

Then she bit down hard on Longarm's tool with her ring-dang-do, demurely adding, "Faster, please. Flora's proddy point about being damned in any case was well taken."

He suspected they'd had that same discussion about the wages of sin in the past, although old Flora seemed the better sport about a three-way frolic. He'd once been invited to bed by a married couple who savored such adventures. But while it seemed good dirty fun to play slap-and-tickle with two pretty gals, the notion of rolling about on the mattress with one gal and another naked man just didn't sound as tidy, although he could see how the *gal* in such a position might enjoy it.

One of those French gals he'd bunked with alone aboard the Divine Sarah's private railroad cars had told him about this more famous lady of the Paris stage who'd invented what she called a *sandwich d'amour,* calling for one slice of female between two slabs of male, with her face-to-face with the gent on the bottom, taking his dong up her cunt, while the other lay atop her back and buttocks with *his* dong up her ass, so the three of them could come together, or try to. Longarm wasn't sure he'd be up to it, in either male position. Nobody but the Mormons, Turks, and Indians seemed to want to admit it, but just one man hogging more than one woman seemed the natural order of things, and from the way gals behaved at such times, it seemed likely they had the same natural instincts.

So he was surprised but not unsettled when the auburn-haired Flora, auburn-haired all over, got up to stride boldly over to join them, sliding under Lili from the far end until she lay on her back in what those French actresses called *la position neuf et soixante,* which described it accurately enough. Both gals giggled when Flora, staring up at Lili's crotch and Longarm's nuts, wet two fingers to reach up and tickle the brunette's turgid clit while she was taking it dog-style. It wasn't as clear to Longarm what Lili was doing with her own head between her frisky pal's spread thighs. But from the way they were both commencing to gasp and moan, he suspected they'd done it before, with or without male company. So after he'd shot his wad and nobody seemed to notice, he withdrew to rummage around on the floor for the makings, then sat in the chair for a bare-ass smoke while the two of them put on a hell of a show for him.

He found it so inspiring that he got up to go over and mount the survivor after he'd about finished his cheroot and when Flora was pleading for a breathing spell.

By this time Lili had lost all her shyness as she gave herself to Longarm the old-fashioned way, sort of, with her head in

133

Flora's lap as the bigger gal leaned more upright against a steamer trunk, petting Longarm's hair while he took turns kissing Lili's pretty little face or one of her mighty pretty tits. Best of all, it took ages to come again, and having his second wind and so much inspiration, he got to try and try, in both of them, until he had to agree they were starting to just show off. Then he wound up seated with a friendly naked opera singer to either side, smoking solo because neither one was willing to risk her vocal cords on even a French cigaret.

But the trouble with kissing a woman to keep her from asking so many questions was that women seldom forgot what they'd intended to ask. So when Flora asked once more what he'd been doing at their hotel if he hadn't had this in mind, Longarm, having argued with women before, said, "I was hoping for something like this. But both you ladies came in too drunk for me to treat you this way with a clear conscience."

Lili toyed with his flaccid dick as she purred, "You ought to feel mortified about the terrible things you just made us do tonight, you sex fiend."

Longarm shrugged—it felt good with a pretty head on either bare shoulder—and said, "I'll study on some other tricks to teach the three of us next time, after I get back from that midnight frolic with that other naughty gal who seems to sing higher than either of you. There's this illustrated Hindu book you have to buy in secret, and they call it the Kama Sutra."

Flora demanded, "Where do you get such notions? Have you been fucking around with some other girls here in Virginia City?"

He assured them they were the only two girls he knew that well in Virginia City, and this was the simple truth when you considered Red Robin had left town and Madam Pearl was a tad old to call a girl.

He said, "After I left you sweet things to sleep it off, that hired gun came in marching that piano player from the Crystal Palace."

Lili said, "Who'd want to mess with *her*? She's tone-deaf!"

Longarm couldn't resist replying, "Don't knock it if you've never tried it. You were both at the inquest. So you heard how I was out in the hall, and only entered that other lady's quarters after she seemed to be in a whole lot of trouble."

"I thought you said he was after *you*," Flora insisted.

Longarm patted her bare shoulder and told her, "If you ever lose your voice I see a great future for you as a prosecuting attorney. They admit women to the bar in some states now. I can't speak for that other gal Jeff Otis was menacing. As you know, she didn't show up for his inquest. I said he was after me because he'd been telling everyone we were at feud and I knew he was a hired gun before he ever tried to point a gun at me. We didn't get to have much conversation after that. So I'm still working on exactly what he had in mind."

Lili began to stroke him as she volunteered, "He was jealous of you. When he saw you were being nice to me aboard that coach, he was afraid the two of us would wind up doing this."

Flora said, "Hey, don't leave *me* out. I think it's my turn. But go on and get him hard for us again if you like."

Lili purred, "Ooh, I like it very much!" and proved it by dropping her head in his lap to purse her moist lips around the head of his old organ-grinder as she went on stroking the shaft.

Flora confided, "She's always got something in her mouth. If Jeff Otis was hired to pick a fight with you, Custis, doesn't that mean the one who hired him may still be after you?"

Longarm patted the back of Lili's bobbing brunette head as he told the auburn Flora, "That's about the size of it, and she's getting it about the right size for a man not to worry about other matters just now."

Flora sighed and said, "I swear, all you men would have killed one another by now if you didn't have us women to worry about you! None of you seem to be able to think of love and war at the same time. We girls are *always* thinking about love. So we learn to worry and fornicate at the same time. Do you think the two of us might be in the same danger as that other girl from the Crystal Palace?"

He said he couldn't say.

She said, "Oh, for Pete's sake, everybody in the hotel knew you were there for that henna-rinsed piano player. The maid who confided in us heard her out in the hall when you had her coming earlier in the day. Now that I've come with you a few times, I can see why she made so much noise. So level with us about those people who hired Jeff Otis to shoot you, damn it!"

Longarm put a hand on the nape of Lili's neck to move her head a tad faster as he croaked, "I don't know if it was people plural, one outlaw I was sent here to identify, or somebody else entirely. Jeff Otis wasn't out to kill anybody in particular but me, unless I read what happened all wrong. I can't say what the *who* he was working for might or might not do. Folks who *hire* guns are less inclined to *use* guns than a cuss such as the late Jeff Otis might. The odds are that my secret foeman won't have the nerve to come after anybody. He, she, or it may have sent for another hired gun by now. I'll cross that bridge when it gets here. But you ladies might be safer if the three of us kept all this friendly shit betwixt just the three of us and . . . You'd better stop unless you like the taste, Miss Lili!"

The small brunette must not have. For she suddenly spat out his dick to spring up, swing her shapely bare behind toward the two of them, then plop back down in his lap to impale herself on his renewed inspiration and gasp, "Oh, my God! Who says you can't bring a man back from the dead? It feels enormous in this position!"

As Longarm hissed in pleasure, and Lili commenced to toy with her own clit, Flora pouted, "That's disgusting! How am I to take my own turn after you've had it up your ass, you fucking Greek!"

Lili laughed and said, "I'm not a fucking Greek. I'm the last of the fucking Irish and it's not up my ass, so there!"

Flora asked for Longarm's opinion. He stared down at the

brunette's bounding tailbone and declared, "Wherever it is, it sure feels good!"

So Flora swung her knees to the floor to bend low for a peek between Lili's thighs before she decided, "All right, as long as it's in your twat, he can put it in me when you've come again."

So Longarm finished in her. It wasn't easy, and he told them he'd see them later, mayhaps for noon dinner at their hotel, if he lived through the effects of all this and that midnight hunt.

They said that they'd likely need to sleep late as well.

As he washed up at their corner sink, it was Lili who said he ought to leave first. He got dressed and did as they were cleaning up. For a gal had more of that to worry about after she'd been screwed, and it took them longer to fuss with their hair.

Fully dressed, walking as naturally as he could manage, Longarm went down to the main floor, where he found it sort of amusing that none of the men fussing with the lights or just jawing seemed to have noticed him going up or down the stairs to the dressing rooms.

But as he waved across the stage to another lawman who'd met his eye by accident, he found his way to the stage door blocked by the brown-haired Miss Miranda, who demanded to know where Enzio Santini might be.

Longarm ticked his hat brim to her and honestly replied, "I can't say, ma'am. He was here a spell ago. I never saw him leave. So there was no way he could tell me where he was going."

She said, "You just came down from the dressing rooms. Is that what you're trying to hide? Were the two of you just up there having a bit of fun, as he likes to put it?"

Longarm raised a brow and said, "Not hardly. I can't speak for any other gent we both know, Miss Miranda, but speaking for myself, I don't go in for that sort of fun with other gents."

She blushed and stammered, "Good heavens! I wasn't accusing you and Enzio of being sodomites! Somebody just said

137

they'd seen Flora and Lili going upstairs. I thought maybe the four of you . . .''

Longarm soberly assured her, "You have my word as an enlisted man I have never in my life indulged in no Roman orgy with your man and those other ladies, Miss Miranda. I swear to you solemnly I have no idea where he might be right now. But I'd be mighty surprised if he came down those stairs with those two other ladies.''

"Ladies? Hah, that will be the day!" snapped the brown-haired gal he'd thought he'd liked best.

That was another reason to keep on exploring the opposite species. No man on Earth had ever chosen a nagging shrew or a wife who'd poison him on purpose. All those horrible hags you saw henpecking haggard men had started out young and pretty, or at least more likeable.

He said, "Ain't neither one of them been all that spiteful to me, Miss Miranda. Mr. Santini told me he'd be coming along on that hunt for that other gal who can hit higher notes than you. If I see him over yonder, I'll tell him you were asking for him. But now, if you'll excuse me, I have to get back to my hotel and change into something a tad less prim and proper.''

Chapter 18

Longarm's Stetson made more sense aboard a horse than down in a mine. So he left his hotel bareheaded, in jeans and shirt-sleeves, with his six-gun riding cross-draw and his derringer in a hip pocket of his jeans. It was crisp at that altitude late at night despite the season. Longarm knew it would be much warmer underground.

He met up with others in the dark near the south end of town. Nobody yelled or shot off their guns. But it would have been impossible for as big a bunch to make no noise at all as they neared the south adits. So the effect on any banshees listening down in the dark should have been an ominous shuffle of booted feet on dusty gravel.

There were three ways down into the bowels of the Comstock Lode. You could walk down long slopes. You could ride one of the ore trams that ran like Frisco cable cars on steeper slopes. Or you could climb in a bucket hoist, like most of the old mining hands, and drop down one of the one-to-three-thousand-foot shafts.

Longarm said he'd just mosey down to the top galleries by way of a ramp. He noticed that a lot of the company police and town lawmen seemed to favor that means of descent.

Longarm's excuse was that he really had no call to prowl way down deep this time. With others guarding that one long and narrow Sutro at the base of the mountain, it hardly seemed likely anyone trapped in the works by this midnight surprise party could get out that way. The fifteen-odd older adits and nobody knows how many try-holes running the length of Virginia City offered anybody playing in the dark after hours that many likely exits to bolt for. With all of them leading up from the top galleries.

When he got to where Enzio Santini and another hand from the opera house had set up two of the limelights near the south working face of the Consolidated mine, he was called over to a trestle table by old Nat Rothfeld. Nat introduced him to a gent named Hathaway from the company police. Hathaway indicated the array of shotguns and boxes of shells spread out on the table and explained, "We don't want anybody firing ball ammunition down here in tricky light with so many of our own in most any direction no matter how they try. We've found these Greener ten-gauges break and reload fast as a Schofield pistol, albeit only two rounds at a time."

Longarm picked up a shotgun, hefted it, and declared, "Two shots of ten-gauge double-O buck ought to stop a bear close in without carrying too far or penetrating too deep."

Hathaway said, "They would indeed. But we're using rock-salt riot rounds."

Longarm didn't argue. The Pinkertons had used rock salt in place of buckshot to good effect in labor disputes. A rioter, a trespassing kid, or hell, a banshee ought to lose interest in whatever it was doing and still not die on you when peppered with rock salt from a heavy shotgun round. And if rock salt wouldn't do it, he still had his .44-40 throwing two-hundred grain slugs.

It was after midnight now. Longarm carried his Greener closer to the quartz wall of the south face and waited patiently until, a million years later, somebody high above them sounded a steam whistle.

Banshee yells were spooky enough. The low dull rumble of hundreds of men stirring quietly on plank walkways way the hell down and down into the mountain felt and sounded as if they were fixing to have an earthquake. Santini and the other limelight hand pumped the pressure higher to shoot beams that would make the sun proud along both stone walls of the lode, about ten feet apart toward this end. Longarm knew that if they kept that up they'd wind up as far apart as the alley out back of most houses and the street out front. The many upright pine pillars of the Deidesheimer frames between were already casting a tangle of inky black shadows out ahead as the teams on each level began to shuffle forward in a vertical line of skirmish.

Longarm stayed put. As it got darker where he was, he could see shards of light shining up through the plank flooring from the gallery below. Bull's-eye lanterns and Davy lamps didn't throw a tenth the glow of limelight. But when enough hands were waving enough of them, you could likely see a good ways out ahead of you and the shadows might not be as sharp and solid a black.

Nat Rothfeld came over to him. The accountant was packing another Greener that evening, of course. But like Longarm, he'd left his hat at home and changed into an old plaid shirt and canvas work pants. He asked Longarm what they were doing there while all the other kids went out to play.

Longarm nodded at the men advancing ahead of them, all sharp black silhouttes now, and said, "I'd like to try something sneaky."

Rothfeld said, "So we'll both be sneaky. What are we doing that's so sneaky already?"

Longarm explained, "If we're dealing with a simple lunatic, he, she, or it ought to scamper ahead of those lights and be trapped at the far end by the others waiting there. If we're dealing with some smarter prankster with some method to all this madness, it's a safe bet he, she, or it should have heard about this banshee hunt before we got in place just now."

Rothfeld nodded and said, "Confidentially, if I was the banshee I'd be somewhere else tonight!"

Longarm said, "So would I. But neither one of us has been gibbering in the dark for whatever reason. The one behind all this is out to scare others away from something down here in this maze. Thinking as scary, I'd duck into some cranny, let everyone sweep past me with all that light, then gibber at them some more from the dark behind them!''

Rothfeld stared off at the now-more-distant glow beyond the skirmish line. "I like it. We'll be where it's even darker, with that banshee between us and the others when they turn around to outline it for us. But you seem to be talking about a *goniff* with a carefully thought-out *plan*! All this *Katzenstimmer* makes a *profit*?''

Longarm said, "I hope that's the motive. A lot of this banshee shit seems senseless. But those old boys who wound up dead were after remote drifts of high-grade, right?''

The accountant said, "Wrong. They were showing a *marginal* profit. By '70 the high-grade ore in this mountain had already given out. Two hundred dollars a ton and up is high-grade. That forty-dollar-a-ton *dreck* Grogan, Flannery, and poor Sullivan were tributing was day labor after you subtract your expenses and the company's share. Did you think we let miners work the dimples and pimples too tricky for more modern methods because we were a bunch of *schlemiels*? The bottom line in mining is to make *money* after your troubles and expenses. There's a *little* gold and silver in *seawater*. Shoot enough electric current through it at a gold-plated electrode and you'll get a tiny *schmir* of extra gold. That's how they prove it's there. So tell me, could I interest you in some Pacific Ocean shares?''

Longarm began to ease forward as he answered, "I read about that in the *Scientific American*. It costs more to generate that much electric current than the gold would be worth. This land is filled with placers and lodes of color too dry or remote to make any profit off. So let's talk about that other blossom rock Boomer Barnes has struck further up the mountain.''

Rothfeld sneered, "*Feh,* what's to tell? By Barnes that's blossom rock. But in the assay office it might run sixty dollars a ton tops, blowing hot and cold.''

Longarm cradled the shotgun, and aimed the bull's-eye lantern experimentally at the far rock wall to his left to open the shutter and shoot a less-impressive beam than either of the limelights out ahead. Then he said, "I heard from one of Boomer's crew that a backer of the Hebrew persuasion was of Boomer's opinion that there could be another bonanza deeper in whatever that is they're digging."

Rothfeld snorted, "I just said what it is they're digging. Just a shade richer than the crust of this established lode. About the same amount of silver with a little more arsenic and gold. The family secret of Nevada silver strikes is that they all tend to be richer near the surface and peter out as you work down. I've heard Boomer's *fahrklempt* idea about being closer to a richer uphill lode. Such a geologist should have schools named after him. But confidentially, it don't work that way. This lode we're inside of right now boiled up a big crack from miles and miles and who knows what, with the metals in the molten quartz bubbling up through it toward the top. Did they tell you the Sutro ran under the bottom of a bottomless dike of quartz? The Sutro runs under the deepest bullion we can afford to mine. So purer quartz runs all the way down to China as far as anyone can prove. If Boomer Barnes knew as much about mining as me, an accountant already, he'd be prospecting somewhere else. Mount Davidson has *had* its big bonanza days. What's left is a serious *business* operation!"

Longarm thought he might have detected movement in the darkness to their left. As he drifted that way, Rothfeld tagged along, but warned, "Watch your step. It's not the fall. It's the sudden stop at the end, and they've been salvaging floor planking where nobody walks anymore."

Then suddenly, as if to prove that nobody sensible would be over that way, the darkness was rent by a high reedy wail of senseless woe!

Longarm threw open the shutter on his bull's-eye lamp to sweep its beam through the forest of uprights between them and the distant line of other lights. The banshee's inhuman wails echoed and re-echoed to where you just couldn't say where they were coming from. Hearing them for the second time, Longarm suspected they might not be so loud, as a matter of volume, as they were shrill, as a matter of nerve-tingle, the way fingernails scraping a blackboard set everyone's teeth on edge far more than a locomotive whistle could blowing a lower note.

Then his wan beam caught a gray swirl that ducked behind a clump of uprights. Longarm crabbed to his left, the lamp in one hand with the Greener in the other like a pistol, while Rothfeld yelled above the banshee wailing, "Be *careful* over that way!"

Then Longarm caught the banshee full in his beam, like a jacklighted deer. Only no deer had ever stared so wildly into a beam of light from under a wild mop of gray hair, waving its arms above the hair, dressed in a tattered graveyard shroud, knee deep in white mist.

"Hold it right there or I'll shoot!" Longarm yelled as he advanced on the unearthly whatever while it went on hollering at him.

Then he did fire, almost point-blank, as the banshee seemed to leap like a wailing ballet dancer and grab for an overhead beam like some infernal trapeze artist. Longarm fired the second barrel as he advanced through the gunsmoke of the first mighty blast to see the raggedy hem of the banshee's funeral shroud where its crazy face had just been!

He tossed the empty shotgun aside and chased the beam of his lamp toward the rocky west wall of the mine as he reached across his gut for his six-gun. Then he was suddenly running across thin air, and let go of both his lantern and weapon to flail through the emptiness, screaming louder than that banshee, as he found himself falling and falling through the darkness below!

Longarm got to find out how those late tribute miners had felt for as long as it took him to get luckier. By a combination of his own forward speed and pure shithouse luck, Longarm managed to grab a cross-timber of otherwise open framework and hang on, boots dangling, as somewhere down below, *way* down below, his .44-40 and that bull's-eye lantern bounced off other cross-beams at what had to be one hell of a ways down!

Above him, Rothfeld was yelling Longarm was dead. That banshee had shut up to let them have the floor. So Longarm yelled up, "I'm not as dead as I *will* be if somebody doesn't get me *out* of this fix!"

Rothfeld moved gingerly closer, shone his own bull's-eye lantern down at the lawman clinging to the rock like ivy, and gasped, "*Oy, Gott sei dank!* Don't move! I'll find a ladder already!"

By that he really meant a ladder to get down to the next gallery, where others were already backtracking with their own lanterns. Nat Rothfeld got to Longarm first. It was still complicated. Longarm had to elbow his way along the splintered beam with his boot tips feeling in vain for some purchase on his side of a three-thousand-foot drop until Rothfeld, having set his own bull's-eye down with its beam trained on Longarm, was able to reach out with one hand while gripping an upright with the other. So between the two of them they got Longarm out of that considerable hole in the ground.

After panting facedown for a spell, Longarm sat up, grabbed their one remaining bull's-eye, and trained it up and up the dark narrow cleft in the ceiling rock showing between cross-beams.

Rothfeld whistled and said, "Like a monkey she must know how to climb! Imagine jumping out over such a drop to grab for a handhold!"

Longarm said, "I just did. Are you packing anything smaller than that other Greener?"

The accountant got his five-shot Manhattan .36 out of his canvas pants and asked if it might do.

Longarm said it would have to as he took the light weapon and put it in his empty holster. Then, as the accountant bawled, "Wait! You can't go up that rabbit hole after that maniac!" Longarm reached up to get himself closer to the ceiling. Then, balancing his booted feet on a beam with his hands against raw rock, Longarm worked his way out over all that ghastly nothingness to where he could just reach what seemed the bottom rung of a rope ladder and haul himself up into utter darkness. All the while below him, Rothfeld seemed to be telling someone else he'd gone completely *meshuggah*.

Longarm wasn't sure the accountant might not have a point as he moved onward and upward in the dark. He didn't know where he was going or how far he had to go. Then one of the ropes of the dangling ladder snapped, to dangle his puckered ass considerably until he'd wedged his knees and back more solidly to work his way higher along the one rope left. The ladder had likely been left to rot in what seemed like an old try-hole. The banshee had to be much lighter than he was, or awfully lucky.

It felt as if he'd climbed a mile, and then it wasn't quite so dark and his elbows were spread out across a wider flat surface. So he hauled himself out of the cleft and rolled clear of it. He could now make out some sky-glow through what seemed a small square window.

He drew the Manhattan and struck a match. He was in what seemed an empty shed. When he rose and stepped outside, he saw it *had* been. He'd climbed out of a forgotten try-hole somebody had slid an abandoned and floorless tool shed across.

He couldn't ask anybody why. There was nobody around to ask. As he stared about at other abandoned structures in the dark, he saw he had acres of Mount Davidson all to himself. That wailing banshee, or anybody working her as a life-sized puppet from inside that shed, seemed to be long gone.

Longarm stared down the slope at the not-too-distant lights of a good-sized town and muttered, "Well, shit, how tough could it be to single out one pest you never really got a good look at from a population of less than twenty thousand at the latest count?"

Chapter 19

Longarm and his fellow lawmen agreed that one A.M. was a piss-poor time to begin a house-to-house search. King Cole said they'd had no better luck searching for High-grade Hal in broad daylight.

That bull's-eye lantern had been busted to hell, but they'd found his .44-40 a few levels down in pretty good shape after bouncing off pine timbers to wind up on a wooden walkway. So Longarm gave Nat Rothfeld's Manhattan back, stuck his six-gun back in its holster, and called it a night.

He caught a few hours' sleep, but rose early at the Taylor Hotel to wake up on black coffee, chili con carne, and a cheroot before he went back to that livery and hired the same paint, Gimpy, despite her off hind hoof.

It was shaping up as a hot day. So Longarm rode north in the same jeans, a fresh work shirt, and his pancaked coffee-brown Stetson with the Winchester saddle gun backing his .44-40 and double derringer.

They were riding through Chinatown around ten A.M. when he almost rode past somebody singing upside down and backwards to Western ears.

It didn't sound like that banshee exactly. But Longarm still reined in and dismounted in front of a Chinese shop that didn't seem to cater to his kind, judging from the window signs being all in Chinese.

He proved that point when he went inside and an old Chinaman came to serve him, blanched at the sight of him, and ran back through the curtains at the rear of the shop screaming in Cantonese.

A much younger and prettier Chinese gal came out, staring at him as gamely as she knew how as she asked in English, sort of, what they could do for him. He had to allow he had no use for the dried roots, snakeskins, and such they had on sale in big glass jars. He pointed with his chin and declared, "I couldn't help hearing somebody singing back there, ma'am. I'd be the law, U.S. Deputy Marshal Long, and that lady still seems to be singing that oddly familiar tune. So I'd like a word with her if it's all the same with you."

The Chinese girl laughed and said, "Me aflaid no can helpee. That phonoglaph leco'd makee sing song you he-ah!"

She saw he seemed confused, so she motioned him to follow her back to their quarters, and when he did he found that old man cowering in a far corner with some scared-looking kids, while out in the middle of the room a wind-up Edison phonograph was still blaring a Chinese song at him through its big flaring megaphone horn.

"You see?" asked the Chinese gal, tossing a rapid-fire aside in her own lingo at her worried family members as Longarm grinned uncertainly and said, "I'm starting to. Is there any way to speed that wondrous new invention up and mayhaps play that cylinder backwards?"

She said she doubted it. But he was free to try. But the best he could manage was reversing the cylinder on its spool so the needle played the singing backwards. The little kids laughed like hell, and it sounded somewhat wilder to Longarm, even though it hadn't made sense to him going the other way.

They listened politely, but didn't seem to follow his drift when he decided aloud, "You could probably get it to play faster and louder by opening up the innards and tinkering with the gear train. But this ain't my machine to tinker with and we'll say no more about it for now.''

He thanked the Chinese folks, got back to old Gimpy, and rode on out to Boomer Barnes's claim.

He found Slim and Porky playing cards on a dynamite case near the adit. Slim told him their senior partner had gone up to the Washoe Valley to see if he could buy some tailored mine timbers and haul them the fifteen miles the hard way. Pointing over at the nearby flume, he added, ''Cocksuckers won't let us use their durned old rain gutter!''

Longarm said, ''Boomer told me. Just when, at what time of day or night, might Boomer have lit out for the high country?''

Porky volunteered, ''Yesterday afternoon. Not long after you was out here, as a matter of fact. He ought to be back by this evening whether he made a deal with old John Hereford or not. He told us he'd sleep over at a place near that big lumber mill on the Washoe. But it's only a four-or-five-hour ride either way.''

Longarm said, ''I may meet him on the trail. You boys wouldn't know whether Boomer owns one of those new phonograph machines, would you?''

They both looked as if he'd asked them whether there was a hot-air balloon on the premises. So he thanked them and rode on.

He figured he was probably riding a fool's errand. When a suspect had an alibi he had an alibi. But alibis were made to be shot full of holes. Gimpy would get him up to the high country in the same four or five hours, and the folks up yonder would say Barnes had spent the night with them or somewhere else. Nobody could be in two places at the same time. So before he wasted more serious study on a man who might be innocent, he meant to find out whether that *could* have been old Boomer playing banshee with them the night before.

Boomer had the motive. More ways than one. Chicken Bill Lovell had salted a forty-foot try-hole near Leadville with a few tons of silver ore from the Little Pittsburgh and sold it as

149

the Chrysolite Mine to Hod Tabor, the senior partner in the Little Pittsburgh. The fact that Tabor had dug down through the salted overburden to hit real color was neither hither nor yon. Chicken Bill had salted the mine with criminal intent, and somebody had been acting criminal as hell out this way.

Longarm wasn't a mining man, but he could still tell a sucker how a few samples of forty-dollar blossom rock could be upgraded to fifty or more, if only to disguise its point of origin. Nat Rothfeld had agreed with that assay man that Boomer's blossom rock had a tad more gold and about the same percentage of silver. The extra arsenic could have been an artistic touch. You could dissolve any metal in aqua regia, a mixture of nitric and hydrochloric acid, and then drip the mixture on any ore sample to leave traces of extra color once you dipped it in alkali water to kill the acid and precipitate the metals out from deep in the pores of the ore sample.

Nat Rothfeld's resistance to the notion of investing in the claim added weight to Longarm's suspicion that no serious investors, Jewish or Gentile, had offered serious money for a quarter share so far. You sold a salted claim for more when you let the suckers come to you. A mining man who spent freely in fancy whorehouses and let it be known he'd turned down offers from some slickers such as Rothfeld or Guggenheim didn't have to name any names or set any prices on shares in his strike. He just had to reluctantly let the bigger mining mogul who bid the highest buy him out.

But before you could salt a claim with doctored blossom rock, you'd need to steal some, and all the remaining rich pockets of blossom in the Consolidated Virginia were being worked by tribute miners you'd want to move out of your way. So by the time Longarm had spent close to four hours in the saddle, he'd just about arrested, tried, and convicted old Boomer Barnes in his own head.

Then he got down off Gimpy near Hereford's mill, up in Washoe Valley, and they told him he was full of shit.

Nobody put it that rudely right off. He dismounted and bet the hostler at the wayside inn just down the log-drag a piece from the much bigger mill complex that they couldn't rub the paint down good and give her all the fodder and water she wanted for a dollar. After he'd lost that bet, he went inside for some needled beer and a casual conversation about recent fellow travelers.

The jovial fat lady tending bar inside said Boomer Barnes had come up the same trail about the same time the day before. He'd left his own livery mount out back, spent the rest of the afternoon over at the lumber mill, and then spent the night with them upstairs.

She said the older rider had lit out early that morning. So he'd likely been tending other chores in Virginia when Longarm missed him at his camp. Longarm swallowed some suds and asked in a dubious tone how she knew the old prospector had been up in his hired room around midnight.

She laughed roguishly and replied, "I wasn't sleeping with him, if that's what you're asking. I'm not that kind of girl, or mayhaps he's not my type. But if he didn't sleep up yonder after he was drinking right where you're standing around ten or eleven, who rode off on his hired horse and saddle this morning? If you missed him or anybody else on that blue roan riding up the trail, it must have gone down that trail earlier. Say he left around sunup and add the riding up."

Longarm did and said, "You're right. Both ways. A man leaving here at dawn would get into Virginia around nine, before I'd had my own breakfast after a hard night. A man leaving here right after you saw him drinking beer as early as ten in the evening would never make it down to Virginia by midnight. Lord, it sure feels good to start all over from scratch, with nowhere in particular to aim for!"

He still got out his notebook and pencil stub to tally what seemed possible. Wells Fargo and the Pony Express had proven a good well-rested critter could cover fifteen miles in less than two full hours, and it was mostly downhill to Virginia City. But a livery nag, in the dark, on a twisty mountain trail? He didn't see how, even when you started from the earliest possible at ten P.M.

He finished his needled beer. The fat gal asked if he planned to have supper and spend the night with them. She looked crestfallen when he told he might eat something first, but had to head back to Virginia as soon as his livery pony had rested enough to carry him downhill. It was none of her business that he was feeling guilty about such a long ride out of the way on a matter that wasn't federal.

He knew that if push came to shove, he could always tell Billy Vail he'd wanted to question Boomer Barnes further about his set-to with High-grade Hal Diller. So far, Boomer was about the only other jasper in these parts who knew the fugitive on sight.

Leaving Gimpy resting out back, Longarm walked the furlong along the Washoe River to the Hereford lumber mill. He had to skirt a quarter-acre mill pond. As he did so, he saw it seemed to serve more than one purpose. One spillway powered the breastwheel that powered the mill's machinery. Another led to a sort of canal lock feeding into the famed fifteen-mile flue washing timbers down to the Comstock Lode. There were a dozen or more milled and notched pine timbers floating on the placid surface, along with a couple of long skinny canoes. As he walked the bank Longarm studied them thoughtfully, then decided, "Naw, there's no way he could have carried that livery mount with him, and unless he had, they'd have found it left behind this morning!"

It sure beat all how a suspect stuck in your head once you'd gone and suspected him. Longarm knew many an innocent man had swung because some stubborn lawman had decided he had to be the one and refused to consider anybody else until it was too late.

If he hadn't wanted to rest his own mount for the evening ride down the trail, he might not have bothered checking Boomer's alibi over at the mill. But he had the time, and the local lawmen down in Virginia could use all the help he was allowed to offer. So he moseyed on over to the office shack, and an older gent in calked boots and a checked shirt came out bare-headed to tell him they'd just hired all the help they needed.

Longarm grinned sheepishly and got out his wallet, saying, "I don't always wear faded denim. I ride for Uncle Sam and I'll show you my badge to prove it."

As he did so he explained his reasons for coming over from the inn. The mill foreman said he had indeed discussed some tailored timbers the day before with old Boomer Barnes. So Longarm would have dropped the matter there and then if the lumber man hadn't softly added as a sort of afterthought, "Cranky old fart."

Longarm put his wallet away as he asked what Barnes had done that was all that cranky. The lumber man wrinkled his nose and explained, "We aim to please, but you have to know what in blue blazes you want from us. We can cut you two-by-fours, two-by-twelves, or most anything up to eight-by-twelves in lengths of four-foot, eight-foot, or twelve-foot. But we have to ask extra for oversized, odd-sized, or uneven lengths, and do you want your timbers hardwood instead of pine, we're starting to get into real money."

"So what did he ask for, seven-foot lengths of canyon oak?" Longarm asked, half joking.

The lumberman said, "Beats the shit out of me. He reminded me of the pests you see at stock sales. The ones who poke at the stock, ask all sorts of dumb questions such as how much milk you might expect from a goose or how many eggs a day that sow might lay, and then leave without ever buying a damned chicken! That old sourdough wasted the better part of an hour with me yesterday about this time, and I *still* don't know just what he's in the market for!"

"Maybe he ain't really ready to buy any mine timbers. He told me the Conolidated Company down in Virginia wouldn't let him use yonder lumber flue. Was that true?"

The lumberman shrugged and said, "I can't say for certain. We own the flue and all the wood and water running down it until it gets to the holding pond down near the Gould & Curry smelter. They have that fenced in and guarded against lumber thieves. Who could blame them? I don't know what they'd say if somebody else wanted to pick up private mine timbers there. Old Barnes and me never talked about that. He was more concerned about dove tails drilled for tree nails, like he was out to build that Mormon Tabernacle or something.''

A steam whistle blew and he fished out his watch, saying, "It's been nice talking to you. But the hands are about to knock off for supper and I have to make sure they all leave for the day.''

Longarm didn't ask why. Any business that made things worth money had to worry about dishonest hands lagging behind to rob the place after hours.

Longarm started to turn away as the foreman moved toward the exit where some mill hands were already crossing the short plank bridge that spanned the mill's raceway. Then he decided that as long as he was up there in Washoe Valley he might as well make sure. How many hired hands might it take to run even a big lumber mill?

He moved over to an empty log carrier just off the path, and half sat on the grounded wagon tongue to light a smoke as the mill hands passed in clumps or one at a time. Then all hell broke loose as one of those mill hands recognized him and vice versa!

"Stop or I'll shoot!" yelled Longarm as High-grade Hal Diller ran back the way he'd just come, shoving other mill hands out of the way, and in one case into the mill pond with a mighty splash.

Longarm sprang up, slapped leather, and ran after him, afraid to fire into the confused crowd of innocent sons of bitches who didn't have sense to hit the ground to either side. High-grade Hal ran for the mill exit, saw the foreman had swung it shut, and ran another way to splash through calf-deep water along the far edge of the mill pond as Longarm, free to fire at last, pegged a medium-distant shot at him and missed him clean. That fall down the mine shaft had thrown the .44-40 out of line, dad blast it! Then High-grade Hal had opened the gates of the lumber flue to wade out and grab a canoe as it was swept through the opening by the current.

"Come back here, you bastard!" Longarm yelled as his man rolled into the canoe to lay flat and whip out of sight, even as Longarm put a bullet into the stern. Then Longarm was sloshing around for another canoe. For two could play at the same fool game if both of them were ready to take such foolish chances!

Chapter 20

Longarm had to wade thigh-deep to grab one squared-off end of a so-called canoe. As he did so, the mill foreman yelled across the pond to him, "What's going on? What's Hank Dalton done?"

Longarm yelled back, "His name ain't Dalton!" before he got too busy for idle conversation. The current closer to the gate nearly sucked him down the flume without the canoe before he could roll up into the dashed-together craft, and then they were off for the Comstock Lode going lickety-split.

Longarm sat up, grabbed his hat brim to pull the sweatband down tighter, and found himself kneeling in the sharp V bottom of what was in fact more like a pig trough than any sort of boat. They were doing close to thirty miles an hour, judging from railroad timetables he'd consulted in the past. But he'd been right about that feeling one hell of a lot faster, with the slightly higher wooden walls of the flue out to fill you full of splinters as they whipped past either elbow.

The Hereford lumber flume ran below ground level across a grassy flat at first, to curve and then follow the course of the Washoe down its flat marshy vale with logged-off slopes rising to either side. But before it followed the natural drainage a mile, the flume commenced to rise on crossed timbers. Or seemed to. What was really going on was that the water in the

157

flume was going downhill at a shallower angle than the brawling mountain stream to the west. The sun was getting low, and the passing scenery would have been sort of pretty in that tawny light if the hills all around hadn't been so bare and the narrow ribbon of water he was navigating hadn't been getting so . . . high!

By craning, Longarm could just make out a distant speeding dot that had to be High-grade Hal in that first canoe. In the short time he'd had to get going, the fugitive was already over a mile down the valley.

Longarm suddenly swore and punched his own thigh, hard enough to hurt, as he experienced that sinking feeling we all feel when we see, too late, what we really should have done just a minute ago.

"We could have shut the floodgate and left the son of a bitch stuck in a dry flume way in the middle of the air!" Longarm groaned, feeling about as smart as a swain who'd called a Miss Mary a Miss Jane in a porch swing.

There was nothing he could do about that now. They both seemed as committed to a fifteen-mile scenic ride, courtesy of the Hereford Lumber Company, and High-grade Hal figured to hit the far end running, with a good-sized town to lose himself in, before this ugly son-of-a-bitching pig trough carried Longarm into the downstream holding pond at the far end. He looked about in vain for some means of making his own craft move faster. There were no oars or poles on the dank V bottom. It was dank because the two big solid sides hadn't been beveled together to be too watertight. Longarm toyed with the notion of making it leak more, in hopes of making this canoe heavier than the one out front. Then he saw that no matter what either rider did, they were moving with the swift current in the flume. No slower. No faster.

He was just as glad a mile or so on when the elevated flume made a tight turn to the east and the water to Longarm's left rose to slop over the side in sheets as the side of his crude craft rose higher than the edge while its V bottom scraped wet wood a spell. Then they were headed at the eastern wall of the Washoe Valley and he saw why. The lumber flume's more level grade had put it higher than some of the bare hills to either side. He was headed lickety-split for a pass through the valley wall. He couldn't see where in thunder High-grade Hal might be in that other canoe now.

Then he was through a short stretch of ground-level canal and way in the middle of the air some more where the flume builders, anxious to keep the water running smooth as well as swift, had run it across the smaller valley beyond on another trestle. Another *higher* trestle.

Longarm told himself not to look down as he stared ahead for some sign of his quarry along the snaking curves of the water channel. It had to snake because, as that reporter from New York had noticed, the eastern slopes of the Sierra Nevada were steep and rugged. If he hadn't felt as if he was about to fall to his death any second, Longarm might have admired the hydraulic engineering he was experiencing. The carpenters who'd nailed all this framework together had doubtless studied the methods of those ancient Roman engineers who'd run water for miles on stilts or through tunnels at a constant grade. Longarm had read how the old-time Romans had discovered your aqueduct got clogged with lime and silt if you ran the water too slow, or torn apart by the current if you ran it too fast. He could see in passing how the flume's builders had had to put fresh planking in during he dozen or so years since they'd built it. The pine weathered to silvery gray where it was dry, or sooty black where it was wet more often. Fresher lumber looked like fresher lumber. It was sure sobering to consider how high off the ground some fresh lumber had been installed. It made a man depending on it for his life consider how they knew any of this soggy wood was fixing to fail before it failed. A few mine timbers spilled over the side were one thing. His own ass was another!

The flume whipped through another pass to veer sharply north to follow a contour line closer to ground level. He saw they'd taken advantage of the lay of the land in this stretch to save on trestlework. The flume ran south a few furlongs to hairpin around a natural amphitheater and run back north along the far side of the deep and narrow glen.

High-grade Hal had noticed that sooner. His canoe was scooting north along the far side, and the distance between them was rapidly narrowing as the desperate federal want opened up on Longarm with his own six-gun!

Longarm returned the outlaw's fire with his own .44-40 as they tore at one another like armored knights in old-time jousting lists. Only they were aiming six-guns instead of lances at one another and neither was wearing armor!

And the distance was much greater. Longarm got the distinct impression something meaner than a bee had just buzzed by one ear, and High-grade Hal suddenly dropped out of sight after Longarm pegged a shot across the way at *him*. Then he'd whipped out of range again, with Longarm still headed south and his quarry carried north by the same relentless current.

Longarm reloaded as he studied on what he might have just wrought. Unless you were Buffalo Bill, you just couldn't say whether you'd done a man you couldn't see when he dropped out of sight when you fired. A lot of dead Indians had popped back up on him in the past. On the other hand, that young enemy boy he'd fired on in the peach orchard at Shiloh had still been lying there when a scared young Private Long had moved in on his position.

"If we got him we got him," Longarm muttered to his six-gun. If we didn't, he'll run for it in the tricky gloaming light with a good lead on us! So where do you figure he'll run?"

His .44-40 had no opinion to offer. Longarm considered that dustup at Madam Pearl's and decided, "No man pays that much to board, with pussy thrown in, when he has a better place to hole up. He asked Barnes for a job and went loco when Barnes turned him down because he was afraid to ask anywhere *else* in Virginia. That's how come we just found him working in a lumber mill half a day's ride west, and how far *east* have we gone now?"

He started to get out his watch. He decided not to bother. There was no way to time a trip when you weren't certain of the time you might have started. That reporter had said they'd made it down to Virginia in thirty-five minutes. As Longarm rounded the hairpin to whip north some more, he decided they should be about halfway there, with about a quarter hour to go.

The wild scenic ride swept him around other turns and across other trestles to where he'd have been turned around if the low afternoon sun hadn't pointed all the long shadows as reliably as compass needles. He whipped through another pass to see High-grade Hal that same teasing distance ahead, just out of pistol or, hell, carbine range. But a killer on the run was a killer with nothing to lose, and so High-grade Hal fired desperately wild shots upstream from time to time. From the outlaw's rate of steady fire, Longarm knew he'd found another quick-loading Schofield of whatever caliber.

Longarm could see the smelter haze above Virginia City against the darkening eastern sky ahead now. He smiled wolf-ishly and growled at the outlaw plunking shots at him, "You go ahead and use up all your ammunition, little darling. I'm saving mine for a more intimate square dance and . . . what the hell?"

His crude canoe was dragging its V-shaped hull along the bottom of the V-shaped flume, slowing down, even as he wondered why. They hadn't taken on enough water to be sinking. He glanced back over the squared-off stern to see there was much less water chasing him down the flume. Even as he watched, the level dropped, then dropped some more. Those sons of bitches up at the lumber mill had shut the floodgate to choke off the infernal flow!

It made sense when you studied on it. He'd told the mill foreman the hand they had on the payroll was somebody else, and they knew *he* was the law. So it hadn't taken them more than a quarter hour or so to ask somebody higher up what to do. And the advice they'd been given made more sense to them than it did to a lawman stuck in a grounded canoe way in the middle of the air!

Glancing wildly about as his own craft shuddered to a soggy

halt in the almost empty channel, Longarm saw they'd almost made it. He could see some of Virginia City around the eroded curve of Mount Davidson the flume had been circling when they'd shut the water off. High-grade Hal must have known where he was too. He was out of his own canoe and on his way down the flume, arms out to either side for balance as his boots splashed along a sort of wide wet tightrope two stories above the sloping ground below.

Longarm gulped, took a deep breath, and sprang up to leap over the squared-off bow and chase his want along the elevated waterway. It was an ass-puckering bitch to keep your footing in a slimy wooden gutter never meant as a catwalk. But he had to try, and if he fell off on the high side, he'd likely pull through in time.

Both runners had their six-guns in their far-flung right hands as they indulged in a foot race that P. T. Barnum would have proudly sold tickets for. High-grade Hal's desperation lent wings to his feet. Longarm's desire to catch the rascal kept him from looking down and losing his enthusiasm. But they were high in the sky in more ways than one, and both were losing wind as they approached that mining claim staked out by Boomer Barnes, with Longarm slowly gaining.

That kid called Slim came out from between the tents with his own weapon as he heard the considerable clatter of boots along wet planks.

Slim ran downslope with his shotgun, calling out for the runner in the lead to stop. High-grade Hal pegged a shot at Slim instead. Then he had to hit the slimy planking as Slim let fly with his ten-gauge.

Neither was hit. But the diversion gave Longarm time to close the distance considerably by the time Diller risked getting back up to run on. When Longarm called out for him to give it up, High-grade Hal dropped back to one knee, facing upstream, to draw a bead on Longarm with both hands gripping his Army .45.

Longarm did a running belly flop in the wet slippery V of the flume with his own gun's muzzle leading the way. So as they both fired, the bullet meant for Longarm's middle whipped over him while the bullet aimed at High-grade Hal hit just about where Longarm had aimed it.

The escaped killer dropped his six-gun to clutch at his chest with both hands as he rolled over the side of the flume like a tired trail hand rolling into a bedroll spread out on the ground. But it was a good twenty feet to the ground, and he bounced off one of the trestle timbers along the way to land as limp and almost as flat-looking as a bear rug.

Longarm reloaded and put his .44-40 back in its holster as Boomer Barnes and the dumpy kid called Porky came running down the slope from the claim. Then Longarm forked a leg over and proceeded to climb down as Slim called up, "Who was he? What had he done? Did you get him or did I?"

Longarm waited until he'd joined the three of them around the mortal remains of the late High-grade Hal before he said, "Let's say we both fired on him and I'll cut you in on any bounty money on this federal want. Your own district court will handle such details. With any luck they'll let me head back to Colorado now. They only wanted me to pick this poor bastard out of the crowd."

Boomer Barnes stared down at the corpse to volunteer, "That's him, all right. We knew one another over in Leadville, like I told you the other day. What were the two of you doing up in that lumber flume, by the Great Horned Spoon?"

Longarm grimaced and said, "It's a long story. Suffice it to say he was working in Hereford's lumber mill up until about half an hour ago."

Barnes gasped, "The hell you say! I was just up yonder. Only got back here this morning. I never saw him around that lumber mill."

Longarm said, "He'd have been working inside whilst you were ordering them mine timbers. It's likely just as well he didn't spot you either. This old boy could sure make up his mind in a hurry. Have you still got that livery mount you rode up to the high country and back, Boomer?"

The mining man shook his head and said, "Not hardly. If

I wanted the bother of tending a horse for days betwixt rides, I'd keep my own here. It's easier and cheaper to just hire a pony for the day. So as soon as I got back this morning I returned it to the livery. Why did you ask?''

Longarm said, ''Two reasons. To begin with, I can't see carrying this shot-up cadaver over my shoulder. I wanted to ask one of your hands to ride into town for some help out here from Deputy King Cole. After that, to tell the pure truth, I was establishing an alibi for you, Boomer.''

The older man raised a brow and replied, ''Well, thanks, I reckon. An alibi for what?''

''Whatever somebody else thought they were doing last night closer than the Washoe Valley. That fat lady at the wayside inn near the lumber mills puts you in bed upstairs about the time I met up with that banshee closer to town last night.''

Boomer laughed incredulously and asked, ''You thought I was in bed with old Martha? That'll be the day. I told you how well I get on with Miss Joyce at Madam Pearl's. The boys told me about that banshee hunt I missed last night. How do you like this dead crook here as your howling spook? We know he liked to steal high-grade ore and—''

''Horses,'' Longarm said. ''I just rode the Hereford flume in a glorified pig trough. Speaking from experience, there's no way either of you could have ridden one upstream or down with a horse. And it's half an hour shooting the flume, but six or eight times that riding the trail on horseback. Add it up.''

Boomer did and decided, ''In sum you're saying it don't look like either one of us old pals from Leadville could be the banshee?''

To which Longarm could only reply, ''That's about the size of it. Damn it all to hell!''

Chapter 21

By the time they had High-grade Hal in the morgue, and did some of the paperwork on how he'd gotten there, the sun had set and then some. So Longarm was wearing his tweed suit against the evening chill as he made his way through the darkness working with another bull's-eye lantern and a borrowed Winchester Yellowboy.

King Cole and the town marshal, Talbot Thurber, caught up with him as he was picking the lock of an engine house up the slope from that tool shed above the rabbit hole he'd crawled out of the night before.

When King Cole asked what they were doing there, Longarm explained, "We found nothing down yonder where the banshee beat me out of the mine by minutes. Unless somebody packed such a toy with all its other gear through town on the run, I'm betting it was hidden somewhere close. This brick-walled engine house with a padlocked steel door is as good a place to hide stuff as I see anywhere else for a ways."

He proved his point a few minutes later. At first sweep of a bull's-eye beam, the engine house contained little more than cobwebs and its rusting machinery, dominated by a long, cold, and empty upright boiler. But when Marshal Thurber said as much, Longarm opened the firebox door to shine his beam in, and almost dropped the lantern when he saw the crazy gray

165

face of the banshee staring back at him from the dark interior.

But Longarm set the lantern on the cement floor and hauled the whole thing out to discover it was, as that tenor had said, little more than papier-mâché with wisps of wig and gray gauze stuck to it. He then hauled out the black rope, a lot of black rope the ghostly dummy had hung from by its head. There was a snap fastener at the far end of the first hundred feet. There were more rope coils further back in the boiler. But that was not the prize. He finally hauled the disassembled Edison phonograph out, along with its detached horn and the big basket, painted black. Then he set the base in the basket and attached the horn and needle arm as Marshal Thurber asked what in the world that wonder was.

Longarm cranked the spring-drive mechanism up as he replied, "They got at least one more of these over to Chinatown. But there can't be a hundred west of the Mississippi yet. Ain't but three or four outfits licensed by Mr. Thomas Edison to make and market his phonograph. I suspect this one's been fiddled with in ways Mr. Edison would not approve."

He put the needle to the shellacked wax cylinder and let her rip. It sounded awful, speeded up with the cylinder reversed to play backwards. Marshal Thurber gasped, "Son of a duck! You've caught the fool banshee, and listen to her *wail*!"

Longarm cocked his head to listen some before he decided, "Ain't as loud-sounding up close as it sounds down in the mine, with heaps of echoes and the impression it's farther away in the dark. He lowered this phonograph in the basket and, see here, turned it on with this other length of black fishing line. He likely let it wail betwixt two levels, where nobody could see it or make out where the noise was coming from."

Longarm turned off the dreadful sound, and began to reverse the cylinder as he explained, "That scarecrow puppet was what magicians call a diversion. It was meant to make the intended victims look some other direction as this speeded-up cylinder rang out through this megaphonic horn."

King Cole opined, "While it scared the shit out of them too!"

Having reversed the cyinder to play right, Longarm just nodded and switched the machine on again. The high-pitched keening still sounded dreadful. But you could tell this time that some lady was announcing something in High Dutch before going into a rendition of an aria by that Mr. Wagner, whose songs sounded sort of spooky and excited even *before* one played them speeded up and backwards in a smoke-bomb cloud.

Longarm stopped the reedy rendition and asked if they'd heard enough. Thurber said, "Lord, yes. I've heard nanny goats sing more dulcet. Now tell us who's behind all this spooky shit and how come."

Longarm sighed and said, "I was afraid you were fixing to ask that. I haven't figured out how anyone I've suspected, so far, could have been the one I was chasing last night."

King Cole said, "You may well have chased him clean out of the banshee business. Come morning everyone in town will know he, she, or it was just a fake, and you'd have to have brass balls and no brains at all to start up again now."

Longarm had to agree as the three of them left the engine house with all the ghostly gear they'd found. Carrying the phonograph down the slope with Thurber packing his borrowed Winchester, Longarm casually mentioned his personal Winchester '73 and that livery paint he'd had to leave up near Hereford's mill in the Washoe Valley.

Thurber said, "They got a telegraph line up to the mill from Gould & Curry. They use it to order timbers and such. We can ask 'em to have somebody riding back down on horseback lead your mount in for you come morning. Nobody would be coming down from there by any means of transportation tonight."

King Cole volunteered, "That trail's a mite treacherous to ride in the dark, and you'd never get me in one of them flume boats in broad-ass daylight!"

So once they'd packed the blossom-rock banshee and all

167

her workings to the town lockup for safe deposit, Longarm headed over to D Street with his borrowed Yellowboy and some fresh ideas.

At Madam Pearl's he found the crowd in a festive mood in the taproom because a skinny young cowhand was atop the bar, naked as a jay, trying in vain to win a twenty-dollar bet while the other men and more modestly dressed whores laughed at his attempts to stick his own dick in his mouth.

He had his head on the bar with his bare ass above it and his booted feet hanging over the end. It looked painful. One of the whores called out, "Close, but no cigar! Would it help if I leaned on your ass, Tex?"

Longarm was looking for that colored gal to announce him when Boomer Barnes came out of the crowd, grinning, to declare, "Great minds run in the same channels. Miss Joyce seems to be entertaining another visitor, but I tell you true, she's worth the wait. Who are *you* out to screw and how come you're packing that Yellowboy, Longarm? Ain't a gal on the premises you have to screw at gunpoint!"

Longarm smiled thinly and said, "I came over to talk to Madam Pearl about mail-ordering."

Barnes blinked and asked, "You want to send away for something by mail from a whorehouse?"

Longarm said, "It's a permanent address. Who's to say what High-grade Hal or anyone else might have ordered by mail from this return address? I nabbed an outlaw one time who was writing home and getting the answers we traced in care of a general store. We just found some shit they were using to scare tribute miners away from color they were after. I can't see buying any of it here in Virginia. So they likely sent away for it."

Barnes seemed to want to hear more. But then that colored maid came by with some towels, and Longarm asked if he could see her boss lady.

She said to follow her on up because *Madame,* as she put it, had left standing orders for him to come up and lay her any time.

Longarm suspected Madam Pearl had meant it when she greeted him up in her quarters with a sloppy kiss and proceeded to shuck the imposing outfit she had on.

He stopped her before she could get out of her black-lace corset and undergarment. He said, "Hold the thought. We may both be fixing to get assassinated."

Longarm moved into the bay window to pull down the blinds as the big blonde gasped, "Surely you jest! Why would anyone want to kill you or me?"

Longarm moved a high-back chair around a lamp table as he replied, "Me for guessing too much and you for knowing too much, most likely. We can talk about it once I set the odds more in our favor."

He took off his hat and set it atop the back of the chair. He had to adjust it some. But now the hat and chair cast a shadow on that window shade that a party outside in the dark might take for a sucker just sitting there like he was tired of living.

Longarm turned back to the confused Madam Pearl to say, "I noticed coming up the walk this time that you have a flat-topped mansard roof on this place. Is there any way you could get me up there?"

She didn't look a lick less confused as she said, "There's a ladder leading up from the attic to a trapdoor in the roof. Ain't this an odd time to consider sunning yourself bare-ass? You *were* fixing to get bare-ass sometime tonight, weren't you?"

He chuckled fondly and said, "I admire a one-track mind when its favorite track leads down the primrose path. But let's go up on that roof first."

She grinned, allowed she'd always thought moonlight screwing was romantic, and led him out to the stairs. He followed her up to the attic tucked between inward-slanting roof rafters with a good part of the center straight across. Madam Pearl lit a candle stub so they could see better, and pointed out a built-in ladder leading up from behind a pile of steamer trunks and old furniture. Longarm moved around them with his Winchester and started up the ladder, saying, "Douse that candle as I'm fixing to open the trapdoor. I like to let the other side *guess* where I might be in a night fight."

The candle winked out as Longarm cracked the trapdoor to the starry sky above. He climbed out to find himself atop a thirty-by-thirty-foot expanse of tarred roofing felt with a brick chimney rising north and south of him. He eased over to the east to find nothing at all in the way of a railing. He dropped to his belly with his elbows near the gut-wrenching drop over the slanting mansard shingles, and trained the rifle east across the lower rooftops yonder.

Then Madam Pearl was crawling on her belly to join him in just her underwear and black-mesh stockings, gasping, "Jesus! I didn't know I owned such a scary roof! It's enough to make a girl's pussy dry up! What are we doing up here, Custis?"

He said, "I ain't certain. But now that we have time to talk, a man with no fixed address here in Virginia might pick up his mail in public in care of the general post office. On the other hand, he might give the address of some local resident willing to let him. Your turn."

She had to consider the full meaning of his question before she nodded her blond head and asked, "You mean besides my girls and me? I don't mind if good customers have their mail or parcel post sent to them in care of this place. It's up to them to explain why they pick up their mail at a whorehouse. But you'd have to ask my housekeeper, Fern, who in particular might have sent what to whom. I don't sweep the halls or wash the windows either."

He grimaced and asked, "Might Fern be that pretty colored gal in maid's livery?"

The gal who ran the whole shebang said, "That's Fern. You're not the first who's noticed she's pretty. But you can't screw her. She's really my housekeeper, and good servants are hard to find. Why do you want to know about other men picking up their mail downstairs?"

He said, "We just found a mess of stuff you'd have a tough time coming by in any local store to begin with. And you

170

might not want any local merchants testifying at your trial. So it's ten to one the rascal I'm after right now sent away for some joke-shop novelties and one of those Edison phonograph machines. If I can prove he ordered some High Dutch opera cylinders as well, I have him in the box.''

"Fern never said anything to me about such unusual mail orders,'' Madam Pearl volunteered.

He said, "She'd have no call to, even if she knew what was in the box, if it was addressed to somebody that didn't live here. I'll ask her later. Right now I want you to crawl back to that trapdoor and wait in the attic west of that pile of steamer trunks.''

She asked why. He snapped, "Do it!'' and she demurely told him to hurry it up so they could have some fun playing in her attic as she slithered back across the flat roof by starlight.

Longarm was glad she had when, moments later, there came a flash of flame and the blast of a gun muzzle from the somewhat lower mansard to the east, closely followed by the crash of smashing glass as Longarm's unseen foe fell for that decoy shadow against the window blind below!

Longarm returned the favor by firing at the muzzle blast across the inky black gulf of two backyards. He couldn't see what effect his own shot had had, because the other rifleman was just a black blur against the flat black rooftop Longarm was aiming down at.

Then that other rifle flashed again to ricochet hot lead off the copper roof-edging just inches from Longarm's head. So the next time he fired he rolled, and that was one ass-puckering experience atop a railingless roof in the dark.

He'd never had time to zero this borrowed Yellowboy in. It was called a Yellowboy because its receiver was cast brass instead of the machined steel of more modern Winchesters. The Winchester '66 Yellowboy lacked some of the punch of the '73, lobbing its similar two-hundred grain bullet with only twenty-eight grains of powder. But this fight was at close range for rifles, and with any luck a gun this old should have had its fool barrel realigned if it needed to be. There was no way to use the open gunsights in this light.

His opponent seemed to be lying doggo across the way. Another muzzle flash might flush him. But the trouble with that was you had to fire at nothing, roll, and lever another round in the chamber before you could fire back at somebody who'd fired, rolled, and levered another round in *his* chamber. There had to be a better way.

Longarm braced the Winchester's barrel on the copper roof trim, and drew his six-gun with a left-handed twist to hold it as far from his own head as he could before he fired it at nothing in particular.

The shootist across the way fired at the muzzle flash. Longarm got off his own rifle round an instant later, to be rewarded with a cry of pain and the sound of another rifle sliding down shingles to the dark yard below.

Longarm rolled up and flew down the ladder and whorehouse stairs to tear out the back door and across the intervening backyards, leaping a fence on the way, and charging up the back steps of that house to the east. It seemed a boardinghouse from the sights and sounds as Longarm tore up the stairs ordering everyone to duck back in their damned rooms for now.

Near the head of the stairs he met Boomer Barnes coming down them, with one hand gripping the bannister and the other the side of his own bloody face. Longarm paused with the muzzle of the Yellowboy trained upward to quietly ask, "How bad are you hurt, Mr. Barnes?"

The grizzled prospector croaked, "Hard to say. Could I have got this far if I really had a bullet in my skull?"

Then before Longarm could answer, the man he'd shot in the head with an underpowered rifle let go of the bannister to come down the stairway at him ass-over-teakettle as Longarm stepped aside lest he get blood and brains all over his tweed pants.

Chapter 22

There was nothing like a gunfight after sundown to attract a crowd. So that boardinghouse was soon cluttered with other lawmen, curiosity-seekers, and of course the folks who boarded there.

Longarm was joined on the landing where Boomer Barnes lay by those lawmen he'd been up the slope with earlier, Cole and Thurber. The town marshal opined, "You sure have been busy this evening. But didn't you just tell us this suspect wouldn't work as that blossom rock banshee?"

Longarm cradled the Winchester and finished lighting his cheroot as he replied, "I did. I hadn't figured it out yet. It came to me as I was wondering how to get my own saddle, saddle gun, and hired livery mount down from the Washoe Valley after I'd left them there to go for a boat ride."

He stared soberly down at the man he'd just shot. "Old Boomer could fill in some blanks if he wasn't so dead and was willing to tell us. But let's say he left the bar in that wayside inn near the lumber mill around ten or eleven, like they said. Then let's say that once he mussed his bed upstairs to make it look slept in, he crept back down to quietly saddle his own hired livery mount and lead it from the stable before midnight. Then let's say he led it down the trail to Virginia a ways, before he wrapped the rein ends around the saddlehorn and gave the pony a good lick to send it running down the trail. The trail hardly anybody rides after dark. What would you expect a whupped horse far from home to do next?"

King Cole said, "Run home, of course. Everybody knows most horses run for the safe feelings of their own stall when they're scared or just mixed up. That's how come horses run back into burning stables so often, confounded by all the excitement."

Longarm said, "There you go."

But Marshal Thurber said, "Hold on. You're talking abut a fifteen-mile run through three or more hours of darkness!"

It was King Cole who declared, "Downhill all the way, with horses able to see in the dark better than us. It works for me. A livery nag hired here in Virginia wouldn't consider a strange stall up in the high country its home. It would head for its own livery stable like a pigeon."

Then he thought and added, "Wouldn't the stable hands have noticed a riderless horse coming in around two or three in the morning?"

Longarm blew a smoke ring down at the body at their feet before he said, "They would if one did. But one didn't. After he sent his livery nag on its way, this old sneak had plenty of time to run over to the Hereford mill pond and launch himself down that lumber flume in the dark. I suspect he'd done it before. More than once. Nobody would see a man lying flat in a canoe when it got to the confusion of the mining complex up the slope. Nobody would be expecting anybody out there on the water after dark. For that matter, he might have been able to roll out as he coasted along the last stretch of canal before his canoe got him to the guarded holding pond. However you want to play it, he got down here before midnight whilst his hired mount was still way the hell up the trail. He'd heard about the banshee hunt planned for last night. He'd only ridden up to the Washoe Valley to establish an alibi. Once he got back he was up to his old tricks with that Edison phonograph wailing Wagner backwards at an impossibly high pitch and that light spooky puppet to dangle down that try-hole. He likely knew of other try-holes and ventilating shafts from poking about the abandoned surface workings. You gents were with me when I found his base of operations in that old engine house.''

Thurber said, ''We were. But how come? I mean, why would anybody with a lick of sense want to dingle-dangle fake banshees down in a mine like that?''

King Cole said, ''That's easy. He was crazy. You know how prospectors get, spending days alone in the wilderness with nobody to cuddle up with but a burro.''

Longarm shook his head and said, ''He wasn't crazy. Just greedy-mean. He was tired of searching for color. So he decided to grow his own. He duped a couple of green kids to dig a hole and staked a mining claim there. Then he dropped some doctored blossom rock in his so-called mine when they weren't looking, and let them muck it up with a little plain old country rock he shot down on it from time to time. He'd soaked his real ore with a brew of gold and arsenic to make it assay a tad richer and, better yet, not exactly the same as the blossom rock left around the tribute edges of the original Comstock Lode. It was slicker than most salting. Mark Twain writes about a salted mine where some of the nuggets had part of the words 'United States of America' stamped on 'em.''

Talbot Thurber, who'd studied the local banshee more as a local lawman, frowned down at the dead puppet master and exclaimed, ''I can see why he'd want to scare tribute miners away from the pockets of blossom rock he was stealing from the original Comstock Lode. But why did he go booger-booger and throw smoke bombs at other crews, or at all of *us* the other night?''

Longarm said, ''To make it tougher to figure what he was going booger-booger about. He only stole a gunnyful hither and yon, so the theft wouldn't be noticed. It wouldn't have taken anybody long to figure it was a high-grading scheme if he'd high-graded it by the ton and had his banshee wailing around blossom rock alone.''

King Cole, feeling good about that other cadaver over in

the morgue, asked, "How did High-grade Hal and that other killer, Jeff Otis, tie in with this dead rascal? Was it all some sort of charade they were in on together?"

Longarm shook his head and said, "Not hardly. That fight up at the whorehouse across the yards was real. The only things Boomer left out was that Diller recognized him as another crook and wanted to be cut in on the con game. He wasn't looking for a job. Boomer refused him for two reasons. He didn't want to cut him in, and he knew Diller was hot as a two-dollar pistol. So when Diller lost his temper and big old Madam Pearl snapped the gun out of his hand and threw him out, Boomer told her who he was so she could tell the law."

King Cole had been paying attention. He nodded and said, "High-grade Hal likely figured Boomer would. So he let out for the high country, and that's why none of us here in Virginia could find him in Virginia!"

Longarm nodded grimly and said, "Boomer here couldn't be sure a fellow crook on the run from the law wouldn't come back for more as soon as he could find another gun. So he sent for his own gun, by the name of Jeff Otis, with a view to having Otis guard his ass and mayhaps even collect the bounty on Diller. High-grade Hal was the only one of the three with a price on his head, albeit all three of the sons of bitches deserved to hang."

King Cole nodded, then said, "Hold on. How come Otis was gunning for *you* if Boomer here hired him to gun High-grade Hal?"

Longarm grimaced and said, "I sure wish we could ask one of them to make certain. Otis was crazy-mean. We tangled on the coach from Reno, and it might have just been a case of hate at first sight, with Otis seeing a chance to build his rep by suckering me into what would have only *seemed* a fair fight. On the other hand, once he had his hired gun from Reno handy, and High-grade Hal didn't seem to be around anymore, old Boomer himself might have ordered his hired gun to gun me."

Thurber asked, "How come? Were you getting warm?"

Longarm smiled sheepishly and confessed, "Not hardly. I'd have never thought to look for Diller up at Hereford's mill if I hadn't ridden up there to check this one's alibi. I'd have never had call to *check* such an alibi if he'd had the sense to pull in his horns and just stay home the other night when he *knew* we'd be sweeping the mine works!"

King Cole said, "Don't be so modest. High-grade Hal Diller was done for as soon as we sent for you, and once we had the one crook in the box, it would have all fallen apart!"

Longarm asked bleakly, "How? Even if we'd captured Diller alive, the most he could have told us was the man who'd turned him in might be up to something. I figured right off that Boomer here was a windy cuss with castles in the air to sell. But if that was a federal crime, P. T. Barnum and Buffalo Bill would be in prison."

Staring soberly down at the dead confidence man at their feet, he continued. "Had he turned Diller in and put his banshee aside for just a few days, he'd have likely gotten away with it."

Marshal Thurber asked exactly what the rascal might have gotten away with. So Longarm explained, "He wanted to be taken advantage of by the bigger boys. He let it leak out that he'd struck a vein of blossom rock and wasn't interested in selling his claim or even grubstake shares in it. He made up rich outsiders who might have tied in with Guggenheim or Schwab, because he knew the mostly Irish silver barons here in Virginia only compared notes with one another. He knew *they* knew blossom rock is usually an indication of harder color that has to be worked with more expensive modern methods. He let it be known he'd turned down an offer of such help for a quarter interest. He didn't want to offer anybody an interest in nothing much. He wanted to sell the whole worthless hole in the ground for a handsome lump sum. So he was holding out for such a cash offer. He knew the prospectors who'd struck the first blossom rock atop the Comstock Lode, including Harry Comstock himself, sold out to bigger developers. We've all heard how Comstock, McLaughlin, and

177

O'Riley sold the big bonanza for a lousy few thousand dollars. So Boomer here was willing to *take* a lousy few thousand dollars. He hadn't invested that much in his confidence game. I'm still adding up the figures in my head, knowing I'll never get more than a mighty rough estimate on some of his expenses. They'll have a record of his filing fee and any ore he really sold to the smelter in hopes of a nibble on his hook. He would have been able to re-invest the money in his scheme. Then there's the record he must have left by sending East for the phonograph and other mail-order stuff.''

Thurber asked, ''How did he find out you were on to him at last?''

Longarm modestly replied, ''I told him earlier this evening. Boomer wasn't the only con man who ever darkened the door of Madam Pearl up on D Street. I only told him I was there to talk to her about letting customers use her whorehouse as a mailing address. That inspired him to whip over here and go up to the roof with his own saddle gun, and the rest you know.''

King Cole said, ''No, we don't. You were telling us about that horse and saddle he left up in the Washoe Valley when Thurber here sidetracked you with that question about this old rascal's reasons for all that skullduggery. I can see how he beat his livery nag down this way. How did he get it to stop at his claim just outside of town instead of loping in, all lathered up, to its own livery stable stall?''

Longarm replied simply, ''He didn't let it. He had time and time to spare after our little game of peekaboo down in the mine around midnight. He climbed out of that try-hole ahead of me. Hid his shit in that engine house, and cut across the slopes above his mining claim and those unsuspecting young hands, Slim and Porky, to drop back down to the trail and just wait.''

He resisted an impulse to kick the corpse as he muttered, ''We all know how tedious it gets to wait all alone in the dark. He was likely cussing that livery nag by the time it finally came along with his saddle, rifle, and such. But once it had, he only had to rope it or mayhaps just soothe it to a weary stop up the trail a fair piece. After that, he only had to circle some more, take more time, and ride into town in the morning to deliver it back to the livery he hired it from.''

''Giving himself what read as an ironclad alibi!'' marveled Thurber, who counted on his fingers to decide, ''No way a man could have enjoyed a nightcap around ten or eleven in the Washoe Valley and been down here at midnight, riding a horse he came in on the next morning. He surely was a slick old rascal, wasn't he!''

Longarm didn't like to brag. So he just shrugged, and Thurber turned to direct some other townsmen up to the landing so they could haul the dead son of a bitch off to the morgue.

That meant more paperwork for Longarm. By the time he'd wired old Billy Vail in Denver, it was too late to even think about catching the evening coach up to Reno and the railroad.

But he didn't really care. Things had gotten too excited around the nearby whorehouse for Longarm to ask for more than his hat from Madam Pearl for a spell. But he'd promised those frisky opera singers he'd come back and play with them some more before he left town for good. So he headed up to their hotel to see if they still liked him.

They told him at the desk that Miss Lili and Miss Flora had gone over to the opera house to look at the scenery they'd finally gotten from the Reno railroad yards. He liked to look at scenery. So he headed that way, noting by his pocket watch that it was going on midnight again.

So he wasn't surprised to see good old Flora and the petite Lili headed his way along the walk before he could make it to Piper's Opera House. They hailed him, and ran forward for a mutual warm embrace.

Lili said, ''We were so afraid you'd left on the evening coach with that mean tenor Enzio Santini!''

Flora just said, ''Kiss me. I'm really hot tonight!''

Longarm kissed her, aware they were out on the damned street, and said, ''I'm sorry about taking so long to get back. I've been busier than I expected. But here I am and I'm all yours for the rest of the night if we could just get inside and up the stairs. You say Santini's left town before opening night?"

Lili explained, "He said something about going into business and not having to sing for his supper. Miranda wouldn't go with the big silly. She's too devoted to her art."

Flora rubbed against him like a kitten from the other side as she purred, "We told her about our little . . . arrangement with you and she said it sounded shocking, but that there were some shocking things she'd always wanted to try and . . . seeing you won't be here in town to embarrass her if it turns out too rich for her blood . . .''

Longarm blinked and replied, "Hold on. Are you ladies saying you'd be willing to have me spend the rest of the night with your adventurous Miss Miranda?"

Lili said, "Don't be silly. If three in a bed was fun, think how much fun *four* in a bed must be!"

Longarm laughed weakly and confessed, "I'm trying to. But I'll be switched with snakes if I can figure out who'd do what, with what, to whom, at the same time!"

Flora gave a mockingbird trill and assured him, "Don't worry. I'm sure the four of us will work something out."

Watch for

LONGARM AND THE GRAVE ROBBERS

239th novel in the exciting LONGARM series
from Jove

Coming in November!